F

\

—

D0513587

I2710951

The Vigilance Man

For twelve-year-old Brent Cutler, seeing his father lynched was the most powerful influence on his young life, giving him an abiding and life-long hatred of injustice of any form.

As an adult, he returns to the town where he grew up as a representative of the District Attorney's office. He finds himself going head to head with the man responsible for the death of his father a decade earlier. There will be hard words and tough actions before Cutler can finally lay the demons of his childhood to rest.

The Vigilance Man

Fenton Sadler

A Black Horse Western
ROBERT HALE

© Fenton Sadler 2016
First published in Great Britain 2016

ISBN 978-0-7198-1897-4

The Crowood Press
The Stable Block
Crowood Lane
Ramsbury
Marlborough
Wiltshire SN8 2HR

www.crowood.com

Robert Hale is an imprint
of The Crowood Press

Typeset by Catherine Williams, Knebworth

Printed and bound in Great Britain by
CPI Antony Rowe, Chippenham and Eastbourne

CHAPTER 1

Seeing your own father hanged is the hell of a thing and likely to have a deep effect upon even the most careless and unimaginative boy. When Brent Cutler's pa was taken out the house and hanged in front of him that January day in 1867, it set a mark upon the child which no subsequent experiences in his life were ever likely to erase. This is how it happened.

The Cutlers were living at that time in the small town of Grant's Landing, on the Arecibo River. The family consisted of Mr and Mrs Cutler and their three children; Brent, who was twelve and his 7-year-old twin sisters. Patrick Cutler, Brent's father, was away from home a lot on business and so from an early age, the boy knew what it was to be relied upon to do stuff around the house. That winter, Patrick Cutler had been away for weeks at a time, leaving his wife and children to get by as best they were able. The family never wanted for food and warmth, for when he returned from his business trips Mr Cutler was always flush with cash money; but the lack of a man about the place was keenly felt during his absences. When, on January 21st, Patrick Cutler walked through the door after having been away for over a fortnight, his homecoming was greeted with unfeigned delight.

'Patrick,' cried his wife, Ellie-May, 'Thank the Lord you're back.'

'Ah, I would've been home sooner, but there was a little matter as detained me. How have these young rascals been behaving?' It was plain that he meant the twins, rather than Brent. There was an unspoken understanding between Patrick Cutler and his son that they had a man-to-man relationship and both knew how much Brent did to keep the household on an even keel when his father was away.

'It's good to see you, Pa,' said Brent. 'How long you back for?'

'A good long spell, or so I hope,' declared his father. 'Leastways, I got no plans for going off again in a hurry.'

They had at that time been living in Grant's Landing for four months or so. On average, the Cutlers moved house once a year; often travelling great distances when they did so. Almost, thought Brent once, as though they were trying to put a deal of space between themselves and their previous home.

'I'm famished,' announced Mr Cutler. 'We got vittles in the house?'

'We'll be eating at six of the clock,' said his wife. 'Can you wait that long?'

'Happen I'll have to!' exclaimed Patrick jovially. In the event, though, he was not destined to eat dinner that day; or indeed ever again in the whole course of his life.

A half hour after Patrick Cutler had returned to the bosom of his family and while he was sprawled in an easy chair, telling the twins some nonsensical tale of his adventures, there came an impatient pounding at the door. 'I'll get it!' said Brent and walked over to open the front door. Standing there was a group of six or seven grim-faced men.

'We're lookin' for Patrick Cutler,' announced one man. 'He inside?'

'Who shall I say wants him?' asked Brent, trying to maintain the customary civilities.

'Don't you tell him nothin', boy,' was the reply. 'He knows well enough what's to do.'

With no further words, the knot of men surged into the house and surrounded Brent's pa. Some had pistols in their hands and one was carrying a carbine. Patrick Cutler raised his eyebrows quizzically as he got to his feet. 'What's all this?' he asked quietly.

'What it is, Cutler,' said the man who appeared to be the leader of the group, 'is that you've been dancing between the raindrops a little too long and now you got caught in a storm.'

'Care to speak plainer?' asked Patrick Cutler, 'only

we're getting ready for our dinner here.'

Another man chipped in at this point, saying, 'We been tracking you all the way from the High Peaks and now we caught up with you. That plain enough for you?'

It seemed to Brent, as he watched the scene unfolding before him, that in spite of his professed bewilderment, his father knew, or at the very least had a suspicion, what this was all about. Patrick Cutler said, 'Let's take this outside, gentlemen.'

'Not 'til we found what we lookin' for!' declared one of the men. 'You got stolen goods here or I'm a Dutchman.'

At that moment, there came the sound of splintering wood from the back of the house, followed by cries of triumph. Two more men came bursting through the door, brandishing sheaves of papers. One of them announced, 'We done found these in that little shed out back. Bust down the door and there they was!'

If his father had showed little real surprise at the arrival of the men earlier, it struck Brent that he was now truly dumbfounded at the sight of the papers being flourished in his face. When he exclaimed hotly, 'I never saw those things before in my life!' the words had, to his son, the ring of truth.

The man who appeared to be in charge of the others took the documents and leafed through them carefully. Then he looked up and said, 'These here are bearer bonds, stolen from the mail coach 'tween

Greenhaven and Fort James. How d'you account for 'em bein' here?'

'I don't account for them no how, 'cause I never saw them before. Someone must've put them there.'

The men stared contemptuously at Brent's father, this explanation evidently striking them as feeble in the extreme. Their leader said, 'That's enough, take him outside.'

Patrick Cutler was disposed to resist at this point, but two men grabbed his arms, while another offered him the barrel of his pistol.

Ellie-May had stood silently up to this point, but now she cried, 'Where are you taking my husband? What's going on?'

The man in charge said gruffly, but with a certain amount of courtesy, 'Best you stay here, ma'am, with the little 'uns. I'm sorry we had to take him in front of you.'

'Take him?' said Brent's mother, 'I don't rightly understand you. Where are you taking him?'

'I'm sorry,' said the man, once more. Then they all streamed out into the darkness leaving Brent and his mother staring at each other; speechless with amazement and horror. The twins were not old enough fully to appreciate what was going on and so were not as affected.

'Stay here with the girls, Ma,' said Brent impulsively, 'I'll see what's what.' Before his mother could forbid him, he darted through the door into the chilly darkness. There was a full moon and by its light he could see the little party moving down towards the *Turn of the Cards* saloon. Trailing behind in the shadows, the boy followed; watching to see what would befall his father.

When they reached the saloon, two of the men went in and returned with a half dozen others who lived in Grant's Landing. The men who had come into the house had been strangers, but Brent recognized those who came out of the saloon. There was Jack Taylor, who owned the livery stable, the fellow who ran the hotel and others whom he had seen about town. What Brent Cutler did not altogether realize was that these men were all members of the town's so-called 'safety committee'.

In those days, many towns did not have a sheriff and the nearest marshal might be a couple of days' ride away. Groups of concerned citizens set up what became known as 'vigilance' or 'safety' committees, whose self-appointed task was to maintain law and order. Later, such men were called vigilantes and it is an undeniable fact that some of these individuals terrorized the districts which they claimed to be pro-tecting. The Grant's Landing safety committee was one of the better examples of the breed.

'Well, what's to do?' asked Jack Taylor, 'I know some o' you boys. What's the idea of takin' of a prisoner in this town?'

The man who had knocked on the Cutlers'

door spoke out. 'You and me know each other, Jack Taylor. You know I'm the nearest thing to law up in Greenhaven. There was a stage robbed, matter of eight days ago. Two men killed, driver and messenger both.'

Taylor listened carefully and then said, 'You ain't yet explained what's going on here. I see a fellow from this town; looks like you got him captive. What's the game?'

'We tracked this man-killer all the way here from Fort James. Word is he was one of the road agents as took the mail coach down. He got here just ahead of us and when we searched his place, we found these.' The man handed a bundle of papers to Taylor, who received them without a word.

After he'd looked through the documents, Taylor said, 'You take a lot on yourself, Seaton. Hell of a lot. Come into my town and start searching folks' houses. You say as these were stole from that stage you tell of?'

'That's right. We come to take this 'un back with us.'

'What d'you say of it, Cutler?'

'I say it's a heap of lies. I never saw those papers in my life.'

Taylor thought this over for a space and then said, 'I reckon you got cause to suspicion him of this. I won't oppose you takin' him back to answer for it.'

As the men surrounding him closed in and began to hustle him from the scene, Patrick Cutler tried to break free and shouted, 'Taylor! I'm an innocent man. Let me tell you about it.' At that moment, one of the party cracked Cutler over the head with his pistol butt, sending the man sprawling to the ground. Taylor and the other men from town said nothing, went back into the *Turn of the Cards*.

Brent trailed along after the men who had taken his pa prisoner; far enough behind that he could not be seen in the darkened street. They moved to the outskirts of town, where they had seemingly left their horses. It was when they reached the mounts that Patrick Cutler's fate was sealed by a trifling oversight on the part of those who had tracked him down: nobody had thought to bring a spare horse for the prisoner. From his hiding place in the shadows, young Brent overheard snatches of angry conversation from the men who had taken his father.

'You chucklehead, I figured you'd o' thought of it....'

'Son of a bitch....'

'Can't take him back on foot....'

'Well, I guess that clinches it....'

The leader of the men, who Brent had heard addressed as 'Seaton', said, 'There's little enough point in shilly-shallying round. We know what this man has done and whether he hangs here or twenty miles away makes no odds.'

'You want we should hang him here?' asked another of the men.

'Less'n you want to travel back with him, and he likely to cut your throat in the night if he gets the chance?'

There was silence for a space and then one of the men surrounding Brent's father said, 'Got a rope in m'saddle-bag.'

'You can't just lynch me without any kind of trial,' said their prisoner. 'This is just what I've been looking into.'

'Looking into?' asked the man called Seaton, 'How so?'

'I'm a peace officer, you fools.'

There was a positive gale of laughter at this absurd claim. When it began to die down, Patrick Cutler said, 'Listen to me, I can prove it.' He got no further because one of those standing near to him reversed the rifle he was cradling in his arms and slammed the stock into Cutler's head so hard that the man fell to his knees. Another mighty blow knocked him out cold.

'Don't have to listen to a heap o' foolishness,' said the one who had silenced Brent's father so brutally and effectively. 'Case is plain as daylight. Let's hang him and be done with it.'

It seemed to Brent, as he watched, that there was indecision on the face of the man who was evidently the leader of the band. But by this time, the rope had been thrown over a branch of the old, dead, lightning-struck oak standing near to hand. A noose had been swiftly fashioned and events had taken on an unstoppable momentum of their own.

Patrick Cutler was hauled, still unconscious, onto a horse and the hang-rope fastened around his neck.

Then somebody slapped the rump of the beast and it was all over, with a man suspended at the end of a rope, swaying gently in the evening breeze.

Even at such a tender age, Brent Cutler felt instinctively that it would be hazardous to reveal himself as a witness to the proceedings and so remained cowering out of sight, the tears running down his face. There was, after all, nothing he could do to help his pa. Brent clenched his fists so hard that he later found that he had gouged four deep half-moon-shaped gashes in each palm. At least it didn't look like his father had suffered; he hadn't so much as twitched when the horse bolted and left him hanging there.

After they were sure that their victim was dead, the party of men saddled up and trotted away. Brent went up to his father and broke down in a fit of weeping, clutching hopelessly at the corpse. Then he dried his tears and went home to tell his mother what had occurred.

The following day, there being nothing in particular to detain them, the family paid a farmer a nickel to let them ride on his wagon to the next town, which had a railroad station. From there, they made their way to his mother's family's home, some three hundred miles away. So great was their mother's fear of what might befall them if they lingered she didn't even arrange a funeral for her husband.

Many a boy, having witnessed the murder of his father in this way by a lynch-mob, would have turned bad and sworn to revenge himself on a society which could tolerate such injustices. Some, though, take the other road and find that such a terrible experience fills them with a hatred of anything approaching mob rule and feel a desire to support the official law and do everything in their power to help it along. This is what happened with Brent Cutler.

His grandparents were wealthy enough that he did not have to work and was placed instead in a good school. He did not neglect his studies, and proved to be an apt scholar. By the age of fourteen, the boy knew what direction his life would be taking. He was determined that when he was fully grown, he would devote himself to making sure that nobody would ever again be treated as his own father had been and that every man and woman in the country should be given the chance of a fair trial when accused of even the most trifling offence.

Mixing as he did with other young fellows whose ambitions extended no further than driving locomotives or becoming cowboys, Brent soon gained a reputation for being something of an oddity at school. In all other respects, though, he was as merry and high-spirited a lad as you could hope to find and so his playmates forgave him this minor eccentricity.

When he was sixteen and his schooldays were drawing to a close, his grandfather asked the youngster what he would like to do next and was not at all surprised to hear that the boy wished to work in a lawyer's office. Had there been enough money, then Brent would have liked to go to law school, but his family's finances were not quite up to such a course of action.

'I'm right sorry, boy,' his grandfather explained, 'but I just don't have the funds to put you through college.'

Brent smiled cheerfully and said, 'You've done enough for me already, sir. I've had an education, which is more than many fellows my age have had. If I can get a situation in an office dealing with the law, I reckon I'll do well enough.'

Old Mr Carter was a corn chandler and he wished to do all that he could for his only grandson. He asked round his business contacts until he heard tell of an attorney in a neighbouring town who was seeking a smart young man to help in his office. After some haggling, it was fixed that Brent Cutler would work for the lawyer for a small, regular sum, until he had mastered the business. Grandpa Carter had made some inquiries and established to his satisfaction that this was a good way into the law for such as could not afford to study at college. After he'd made the necessary arrangements, he sent for his grandson and told him, 'Well, boy, I'm happy to tell you that you are provided for and will, I hope and pray, do your duty. Work hard and carry on with your studies and there's no reason you shouldn't go into law on your own account after a few years.'

So it was that at the age of sixteen, Brent Cutler left his family and went to live on his own account. The man to whom he was apprenticed was a hard but fair taskmaster and it didn't take the young man long to discover that he had a positive aptitude for the law. For four years, he learned as much of the law as was possible in a small, provincial town. Soon after his twentieth birthday, he applied for a position at the District Attorney's office, up at the county seat. To his immense surprise, he was successful. It looked both to Brent Cutler and to those around him that his future was assured and that the young man was on his way up in the world.

CHAPTER 2

It had been a good hanging. In fact, sitting now at his ease in the comfortable and well-appointed parlour of his home, Mark Seaton could not recollect a better. He was certainly in the best possible position to judge such things, having officiated at well over a hundred executions over the last fifteen years or so. As head of the Greenhaven vigilance committee, this was his duty. Although he didn't much like taking any man's life, Seaton would allow that he felt a certain sober satisfaction in dispatching wrongdoers in this way. An eye for an eye, it said in the Good Book and as a God-fearing man, Mark Seaton conceived it to be his duty to see that malefactors received their just desserts; at least if their crimes had been committed in or around Greenhaven. In a very real sense, he was the law in those parts and had been so almost since the little town had been founded.

Although a strict temperance man these past twenty

years, at times such as this, Seaton sometimes thought that he wouldn't mind celebrating with a glass of liquor. Instead, he took from his pocket a newspaper article which had been published the previous week and decided to read through it once more. The piece had given him no little pleasure and although he knew it was sinful to surrender to pride, Seaton thought that he could justifiably permit himself a moment or two to experience that glow of Godly content, which is the only reward a truly righteous man needs.

Reaching into his vest pocket, he extracted a piece of folded, flimsy paper. It was from the May 15th 1879 edition of the *High Peaks Plain Dealer; Incorporating The Kent County Agricultural Gazette and Advertiser.* The article, which had brought such a warm feeling to the heart of the leader of the Greenhaven vigilance men, read as follows:

The Town Which Needs No Sheriff

As civilization continues its inexorable march westwards across our fair nation, establishing courts of law, police forces, hospitals, manufactoriesand churches in its wake, we are pleased to say that one town in our own county still shows no need for such blessings as a properly constituted judiciary and police force. The safety committee of the little town of Greenhaven still administers the law, just as it has since the War Between the States.

Mr MARK SEATON, the well-known business-
man, still leads the vigilance men with as much vigour
as ever he did. They say that the District Attorney
for Kent County is determined to see a regular peace
officer operating in every part of his bailiwick by the
end of the year. It is devoutly to be hoped that he leaves
Greenhaven out of the reckoning, abiding by that hoary
old piece of folk wisdom which urges against the folly of
meddling with machinery or institutions when they are
already working very well.

Seaton set the article down on the table with a view
to putting it in the scrapbook which he kept of such
cuttings; a small vanity which he permitted himself.
There was a soft and respectful tap upon the door.

'Come in, Eulalie,' said Seaton quietly, 'the door's
open.'

The middle-aged cook-come-housemaid entered
the room and handed Seaton a letter, saying, 'A li'l boy
done brung it, sah. Mail coach come in early.'

'Thank you, Eulalie. I shan't need you further
tonight.'

'Thank *you*, suh. I 'spects I'll be seeing you in the
mornin'?'

'Yes, God willing. Goodnight.'

'Goo'night, suh.'

After Eulalie had left him, Seaton sat for a while,
lost in thought. The man they had hanged that day had
been taken red-handed in the act of stealing livestock

on a local farm. There could be not the slightest doubt as to his guilt and he had made no attempt to deny that he was one of a gang of rustlers. When the fellow had been brought before him, Seaton had hinted that his life might be spared if he were to cooperate fully and tell all he knew about the rustling which currently plagued the area; an offer which was declined on the spot. Although he knew where his duty lay, the head of Greenhaven's safety committee felt a grudging admiration for a man who displayed such loyalty to his comrades. When informed of his fate, the man, whose name was even now unknown, made one curious request. He asked to be allowed to stand, rather than sit on the horse during his hanging.

Men hanged on horseback or jerked to Jesus at the end of a rope hauled on by a necktie party tended to die hard; kicking and choking for several minutes until they lost consciousness. A man falling from the back of a horse with a rope round his neck stood at least a chance of breaking his neck and dying more cleanly. Since the man about to hang had behaved decently and made his request without any cursing or blaspheming, Seaton acceded to it. Once he was standing on the horse's back with the rope in place the condemned man wasted no further time; without giving any indication of his intention, he leaped high in the air. His neck snapped with an audible crack as he reached the end of the rope and so he suffered not a whit.

Lost in his reverie, Seaton suddenly recollected the

unopened letter in his hand. He broke the seal and unfolded the sheet of paper within. It read as follows:

District Attorney's Office
147 Main Street
Pharaoh
Kent County
5.18.79

Dear Mr Seaton,

You are no doubt aware that it is the devout hope of our new governor to apply soon for state-hood and entry to the Union on those terms. As part of the conditions for such a process, it is of the greatest importance that the rule of law should be firmly established across the whole of our territory; and that with the greatest celerity.

As an integral part of this grand enterprise, the District Attorneys in every county have now been charged with ensuring that a legally constituted sheriff is, in the future, responsible for law enforce-ment in all towns across the entire area of this territory. While cognizant of, and most grateful for, your own informal efforts in the maintenance of good order in and around the municipality of Greenhaven, it is now hoped to arrange for the election of a sheriff in that town.

I am accordingly notifying you that my assis-tant, one Brent Cutler, will soon be arriving at

Greenhaven. As the unofficial leader of your town's vigilance committee, I am confident that you will extend every courtesy to Mr Cutler and provide him with any necessary facilities for the execution of his duty. I need hardly mention that Mr Cutler enjoys my complete confidence and is empowered to make any decisions in this matter on behalf of this office.

I have the honour, sir, to remain your humble servant,

Thomas J. Delaney

(District Attorney for Kent County).

Seaton had to read the letter through twice and even then he could not quite take it in. He had been running Greenhaven as a more or less benevolent despot for so many years now, that he honestly could not believe that his reign might be about to come to an end.

The railroad car was comfortable enough, but so engrossed was Brent Cutler in the papers he was going through, that he might have been sitting on a bed of nails and not noticed any discomfort. When he was on a mission such as this present one, Cutler's mind was wholly and absolutely engaged with the task in hand. He didn't even hear the conductor asking to examine his ticket and the white-bearded oldster had to ask twice and then tap Cutler on the shoulder as well in order to elicit any response.

'I do beg your pardon,' said the young man, embarrassed at the thought that he might have appeared to be ignoring the conductor, 'I was so bound up in all this, I guess I was deaf to the world.'

'Not to worry, son,' said the old man, 'I get that way myself when I'm reading something gripping. Any chance o' seein' your ticket to ride?'

'Yes, of course.' Cutler fumbled in his pocket and eventually withdrew the pasteboard rectangle. He handed it to the conductor, who eyed it curiously.

'Goin' to Fort James, hey? That's a dead and alive little place since the war. What's a young fella like you heading there for, if'n you don't mind me askin'?'

Since the old man seemed disposed to be chatty, Cutler thought it would be ill-mannered and ungracious to snub him and so he reluctantly put down the papers he was holding and said, 'Well, I don't really aim to stay there. It's just the nearest stop to Greenhaven, which is where I'm going.'

'Greenhaven! Now there's a strange burg and no mistake. You mind your step there.'

'Now why do you say that?' asked Cutler curiously. 'Something wrong with the place?'

'No,' said the man slowly, pushing back the peaked cap he wore and scratching his head thoughtfully, 'I don't know that I'd exactly say that there's anything *wrong* with Greenhaven....'

'What then? Come, you can't just let drop a hint like

that and not tell me what's what.' Brent Cutler smiled engagingly at the older man and said, 'Listen, why don't you take the weight off your feet for a space? Sit down opposite and tell me about Greenhaven. Really, I'm right interested!'

There was something so fresh-faced, honest and open about the well dressed and polite young man that the ticket collector acceded to the request and, in defiance of company policy, took off his hat and plonked himself down in the seat facing the youngster. 'Thing you need to know 'bout Greenhaven, is that only one man there counts for aught. Fellow by the name o' Seaton. Mark Seaton. Runs the whole place, more or less single-handed. Leads a bunch of vigilance men. Anybody sets a foot out o' line, those boys kind of tend to them, if you take my meaning.'

'You mean they're like the law in those parts?'

'You might say so. They say as Seaton's a God-fearing man, hot for the Lord and so on. Some of his men though....'

'Yes...?' said Cutler, intensely interested in what the old man was saying. 'They're what?'

'Let's just say I heard that some aren't quite as God-fearing as their boss. Then there's those among 'em who aren't above a little larceny themselves, when nobody's looking. But I can tell you now, Greenhaven's safer than any place you ever went in your life. A woman can walk down the street there, any hour o' the day or night without fear of being molested. There's no drunkenness, no thieving, no riotous behaviour; nothin' at all allowed in the town limits. Quietest and most respectable town you could hope to find. Mind, it's not somewhere I'd care to live myself. I'm not a one for too much preaching and folk being quiet and religious all the time.'

Brent Cutler chuckled. 'I know just what you mean. Even good people need to ease up a little from time to time. It doesn't do to keep too tight a rein on things.'

When he had arrived in Greenhaven in the early years of the War Between the States, Mark Seaton had found a little town which rivalled the Biblical Cities of the Plain for filth and wicked behaviour. Fact was, at that time Greenhaven would have given Sodom and Gommorah a good run for their money when it came to crime and general immorality. The town was ideally situated to be a centre for the smuggling of liquor, running of guns, prostitution and the Good Lord above knew what-all else.

In 1863, the year that he arrived in Greenhaven, Seaton had been just thirty years of age. He was originally from New York, where he had been working as an attorney. The experience had disgusted him beyond all measure. He had seen men as guilty as Cain walk free from courtrooms in which they had been on trial for murder. Compelling though the evidence might have been, a little judicious bribery or, when that failed, threats of violence against members of the jury worked wonders. Even the courts appeared to condone such goings on, allowing wealthy men bail and incarcerating those too poor to post bonds. Mark Seaton had come out West in the hope of finding a simpler and cleaner way of life.

At first, Seaton had hoped to set up as an attorney in some new town, but it hadn't taken him long to find that there was even more corruption in the frontier towns than in the big cities of the eastern seaboard. He had finally ended up in Greenhaven, where he had abandoned all hope of practising as an honest lawyer and settled down as a general trader.

With the small capital that he had brought with him, he prospered, dealing first in the buying and selling of the placer gold being discovered around the High Peaks and then branching out into other merchandise. It was only natural that, as a successful businessman and educated man, he should after a while become the driving force behind the setting up of Greenhaven's first safety committee. Despite the money flowing into the town from prostitution and the traffic in guns and liquor, many of the folk living thereabouts wished for a quieter life; a place where they could raise their children safely. Slowly but surely, by means of a few hangings and a greater number of beatings, combined with the occasional tarring and feathering, Greenhaven became a good deal less rough and ready.

Of course, the craving for hard liquor, free money

and easy women doesn't go away just because some reforming zealot takes charge of law and order. All that happened was that a lot of the less savoury aspects of life in and around Greenhaven became invisible to sight. But even Seaton's enemies had to concede that the streets were safer now than they had been before his arrival and that outwardly at least, Greenhaven was now looking like a respectable little town.

Fort James had, during the war, been an important outpost for the Union army. A thriving town had grown up in the lee of the army base, but with the cessation of hostilities, the soldiers had left and the town began its slow decline. Everywhere he looked, Brent Cutler could see the signs and symptoms of decay and he guessed that in another ten years or so, this would be a ghost town. In the meantime, though, it was fortunate that the livery stable was still doing business, after a fashion.

'Any chance of hiring a mount?' asked Cutler of the seedy-looking youth who was evidently in charge of the stable.

'It could be so,' admitted the young man. 'Cost you, though.'

Brent Cutler laughed. 'Well, I surely didn't expect to get a horse for nothing. Can you hire me out tack as well?'

'Sure. Cost you extra, mind.'

'Sun'll be setting soon. Why not show me your horses and we can settle matters this side of nightfall?'

There were two horses to choose from; both were scrawny beasts who looked as though they might have been rescued from a soap manufacturer's a few seconds before being rendered down into fat. 'They all you got?' asked Cutler in dismay. 'I never saw such sad-looking creatures. It's ten miles to Greenhaven. You sure one of these'll make it?'

The boy shrugged, saying, 'They's the only critters we got. Take 'em, leave 'em, it's all one to me.'

'I'm guessing you're not being paid on commission,' said Cutler sourly. 'All right, what will you charge for a week's hire?'

So astoundingly great was the sum quoted, that Cutler almost choked. Before he could reply, the youth began to mumble, 'Take—'

'Yes, I know,' interrupted Cutler, 'take it or leave it. You ain't much of a salesman, you know that?'

It lacked only a half hour or so before sunset by the time the sorry piece of horseflesh was tacked up and ready to go. Brent Cutler was happy enough to take a leisurely trot by moonlight, though, and had no special desire to waste a night in Fort James.

It was a beautiful evening and the full moon made the road as easy to travel along as though it were daytime. From all that he had been told, Brent Cutler thought it unlikely that he would encounter any road agents in the vicinity of Greenhaven and so he wasn't unduly alarmed when he saw a group of four riders heading along the track towards him. Like as not, they were just travellers, like he himself. It wasn't until they drew nearer that he realized that all the men had neck-erchiefs pulled up over the lower half of their faces in the approved style of wrongdoers across the whole of the territory. His heart sank, because he was unarmed – apart from a little muff pistol he had tucked away in his vest pocket. This would, he thought, be worse than useless against four determined men. He reined in and waited to see what turn events were going to take next.

The letter from the District Attorney disturbed Mark Seaton so greatly that he had to go for a walk to burn off some of the nervous energy which was making his heart race. There is a problem when a man is so sure that his own actions and desires coincide in every particular way with those of the Lord God. If one isn't careful, it isn't so long before you start to think that any kind of opposition to your own actions is really rebellion against the Lord himself. Seaton was a man in this condition; having run the town of Greenhaven for so long, using only the Bible as his guide, the idea now of somebody else being elected to supervise the law hereabouts seemed little short of heresy!

In addition to representing the forces of law and order in town, Seaton was also a lay preacher at the chapel. This meant that during the week he was instru-mental in enforcing his own strict code of ethics, while on the Sabbath he expounded the Deity's view on the matter. These two roles had, over the years, become inextricably mingled together in his mind, until he had begun to see himself as roughly comparable to some Old Testament prophet; one of the Judges perhaps, like Joshua or Barak.

After walking briskly and fairly aimlessly for a half hour, Seaton directed his steps to the smithy, where a particularly reliable and devout member of both the chapel and safety committee had his workplace. Ezra Stannard greeted the head of Greenhaven's vigilance men respectfully. 'Good evening to you, Mr Seaton. I 'spect as you're surprised to find me working my bellows at this hour of the day?' It was past ten o'clock.

'Ezra, I know you as a man who likes to keep his hands busy and his mind pure.'

'Ain't that the truth. You know they say as the Devil makes mischief for idle hands.'

'So I've heard, so I've heard. Ezra, we have a problem.'

'Problem? Nothing you can't reason out, Mr Seaton, I'll warrant.'

'You trust me, I reckon?'

'Mr Seaton, sir, I trust you more 'an any man living.'

'That's the spirit. I need you to undertake a little job of work for me. It might sound a little odd, but I need you and some two or three more to do something without asking too much about the reason why. Would you trust me to that extent?'

Ezra Stannard wiped his hands on a piece of old rag and then walked up to Seaton and thrust out a muscular and calloused paw. He said, 'Mr Seaton, I'd follow you to hell if you asked it. There's others feel the same way. You made this town what it is. Just ask and we'll do whatever you say.'

Seaton grasped the other man's hand and said, his voice husky with genuine emotion, 'I knew I could count on you. There's a bunch of high-faluting types up in Pharaoh, think they know better than us how a town should be kept clean for decent folks. They're sending some fellow down this way to take over the running of Greenhaven and give it over to some shyster lawyers up at the county seat and suchlike. All of us who know what's right must stick fast together and show them the error of their ways.'

'Just set me on the right path, Mr Seaton,' said the blacksmith, 'and you'll see I won't turn back 'til the job's done.'

'By my reckoning, this fellow's like to be coming to Fort James tomorrow evening by the Flyer....'

CHAPTER 3

When the riders were some fifteen feet away, they halted and one of them, a burly man, as large and hairy as a bear, said in a gruff voice, 'Tell us your name, stranger.'

'My name's my own,' said Cutler stoutly. 'What's it to you?'

'It's this,' replied the man, 'there's four of us and one of you. You best do as you're bid. Happen your name's Cutler. If so, then you best hand over any papers you have.'

So unexpected was this request, that Brent Cutler was momentarily taken aback. He had thought that his wallet or watch might be demanded of him, but why the Deuce would anybody be after the documents he was carrying in his saddle-bag? 'That's a blazing strange request,' said Cutler, wonderingly. 'What game is this?'

'It's no game,' said another of the masked men,

drawing a pistol and pointing it in Cutler's direction. 'Wouldn't call it 'xactly a request, neither. Taking it now that you are Cutler, just you do as you're told.'

Mark Seaton's instructions had been very clear. The man called Brent Cutler was not to be harmed, but he was to have all his belongings taken; most especially any documents or papers. Then he was to be stripped buck naked and deprived of any means of transport. In such a way, thought Seaton, any attempt to impose a sheriff on Greenhaven might be frustrated – at least temporarily.

In fairness to Seaton, it must be said that self-interest and the desire to maintain his hold over the town were not the chief considerations motivating his actions in this matter. He was genuinely worried that if once there was an official system for keeping the peace, then it would not be long before all the corruption and graft that he had known in New York would creep into the town. As things were, justice was executed swiftly, with no shilly-shallying or opportunities for crooked lawyers or judges to set free a guilty man. There was often only a matter of hours between the commission of a crime and catching a rustler or man-killer and stretching his neck. If a sheriff were to be involved then there would be endless delays, appeals, bribery, escapes and the Lord knew what-all else. For Seaton and his band, the present arrangement was the neatest possible and needed no improvement. Add to all that the fact that there was scriptural authority for such a system and it was plain to some members of the safety committee that God wanted them to carry on after the present fashion and to have no truck with sheriffs or courts of law.

Meanwhile, Brent Cutler was weighing up the advantages and disadvantages of pulling out his little muff pistol and letting fly at the men who were menacing him. He decided that he had not yet reached that final extremity and so, being reluctant to start a bloodletting over a sheath of papers from the District Attorney's office, he thought he'd let them go without a fuss. He said, 'You really want my documents, then you can have them. I'll be needing to turn round to fish them out the saddle-bag, mind. Don't go getting itchy trigger fingers, hey?'

'Just don't move too fast is all,' said one of the men facing him, his voice muffled from the cloth covering it.

Very slowly and carefully, Cutler twisted round in the saddle and undid the straps on the saddle-bag. He was keenly aware all the while that there was at least one gun pointing at his back. He had led a peaceful and uneventful life up at the county seat and being held up and robbed in this way was the most exciting thing that had happened to him since he was a child. He didn't think that he was in any real danger from these riders, who somehow had the air of ordinary men rather than ruthless outlaws. Not that Cutler had any sort of experience of bandits and killers. It was just that these fellows seemed so unexceptional and down to earth. He found it impossible seriously to entertain the possibility that they might be about to gun him down.

Once he had handed over all the documents from his saddle-bag, one of the riders having walked his horse forward to receive them, matters took a more sinister turn. When the man who had taken the bundle of papers from Cutler had backed his horse away and rejoined his three companions, the big man who had first spoken said, 'Now you can get down from your horse.'

'You want me to dismount? Why? I gave you what you wanted.'

'Not so much talk. Just get down.'

It was at this point that Cutler began to be alarmed about the direction that events were moving. As he swung himself from the saddle, he reached into his vest pocket and slipped the derringer into his palm. He might be the mildest and most law-abiding of individuals, but he had not the least intention of allowing himself to be shot down on the highway without putting up any resistance.

There were only two shots in the little pistol and the ridiculously tiny barrel meant that it would not be accurate beyond ten or twenty feet, but Cutler was thinking now that things were more perilous than he had at first apprehended. This suspicion was amply confirmed when the big man who appeared to be in charge of the riders announced, 'Now take off your clothes!'

'You say what?' asked Cutler in amazement.

'I said take off your clothes.'

'I'll be damned if I will!' declared Cutler. 'I tell you now, I won't do it.'

'Enough o' the cursing,' said the man who had directed him to strip, and it was at that point that things suddenly went very rapidly wrong.

Honestly believing that these men intended to take all his belongings and then kill him, Cutler cocked the muff pistol with his thumb. At the same moment, sensing his reluctance to comply with their demands, the four riders began to move forward, crowding him. Fearing for his life, the young man pulled the trigger of his little pistol, not really aiming at anybody in particular and half thinking that the sound of a shot alone might cause the men pressing in on him to back off. The results exceeded all his expectations, because as soon as he fired, the burly man who had first spoken fell back at once, sliding from his horse. So effective had his manoeuvre been, that Cutler loosed off the other barrel, with similarly satisfying consequences. The man who had earlier been pointing a pistol at him gave a hoarse cry and dropped his gun.

Although he had never yet been involved in such lively events, having only ever worked in law offices, Brent Cutler was no sissy and had a deep detestation of crime in all its manifestations. Before the echoes of his shots had died away or the smoke had had a chance to dissipate, Cutler darted forward and snatched up the pistol that one of the men in front of him had let fall. He drew down on the men and said, 'I reckon the boot's on the other foot now. You fellows get down from your horses.'

'I can't get off my horse,' said the man who had dropped his pistol. 'You done shot me. I'm hurt real bad.'

'Well, I'm sorry for it,' said Cutler sincerely, 'but you waylay and rob a man, you got to expect trouble.'

The other two men slowly and reluctantly dismounted, keeping a wary eye all the while on the young man pointing a gun at them. One of them said, 'You killed our friend. You're like to hang for this night's work.'

'I hang?' exclaimed Cutler in amazement. 'You men shouldn't have held me up. It's as clear a case of self-defence as ever I heard tell of.' Seeing that one of the men was about to speak, he continued, 'I won't debate with you on this. You two who can walk, just you go on down the road. Leave your horses here.'

It was perfectly plain to the riders who had accosted him, that here was a young man who was quite prepared to stand up for himself against all comers. They none of them had expected any serious trouble. Although Ezra Stannard hadn't told them precisely what was going on, they had understood that their action tonight was to be in the nature of a warning, rather than a punishment. However, their friend Ezra, the blacksmith, now lay dead and another man looked to be severely wounded. For all that they had been cautioned against harming this fellow, their thoughts now were bent on vengeance. For the time being, though, there seemed little enough to be done other than to obey their instructions and to leave the scene on foot.

After he was sure that the two men had moved far enough away that they would not be able to impede his actions, Cutler said to the man still seated on his horse, 'Have you another weapon, apart from this one that you dropped?'

'No,' replied the man and followed this up with a prodigious groan. 'You hurt me bad. I think I'm like to die.'

'I'll help you down from your mount, but I tell you now, don't play me false. I'll have the muzzle of this pistol pressing against your body and I won't hesitate to shoot.'

It was no easy task to ease down the heavy man from his horse and he gave several sharp cries of pain before he was laid safely on the ground; but eventually, the thing was accomplished. The two men who Cutler had instructed to walk away on foot had halted on a nearby ridge, where they were silhouetted against the sky. Paying no more attention to the man he had assisted, Cutler set to work untacking the horses of the those who had attempted to rob him. He had, as a boy, worked for a time in a livery stable and so found this a simple enough operation. When his exertions in that field were completed, he foraged about in the saddle-bags until he found a sharp knife. With this, he cut through various straps and reins, ensuring that even if any of the men recovered their horses, then their tack would be in no fit state to be used. Having done this, he turned to the injured man, who was now moaning more or less constantly from the bullet wound in his stomach. Cutler said, 'I told you I was sorry I shot you and I am. I'm leaving now. Your partners are waiting up yonder and I dare say as they'll come to your aid, once I'm gone.'

There was no reply to this and so Cutler slapped the rumps of the horses, sending them running off into the night. Although they could surely see what he was doing, the two men watching him from about a quarter of a mile away, did nothing. They could hardly start firing down at Cutler without running the risk of finishing off their friend or shooting their own horses. When he was confident that he had made it impossible for the others to pursue him, Cutler mounted his own horse and set off across country. He didn't think that it would be prudent to remain on the road that night, just on the off chance that the men he had encoun-tered had associates prowling around nearby.

Brent Cutler was no fool and the more he mulled over the events of the last hour or so, the stranger they appeared to him. Because of the excitement of the thing, he had scarcely had a chance to think about what had taken place until now. As he did so, his horse plodding along patiently through the darkness, he gradually came to see that this had been no bungled robbery by a bunch of road agents. He had known instinctively, by the way that they had spoken, that these were not rough outlaws, but rather ordinary, respectable men. The man he had killed had even reproved him for cursing; was that likely behaviour from a bandit?

In addition, there was the indisputable fact that they had known his name. That was exceedingly peculiar in itself. Taken in conjunction with the fact that their first and foremost interest had been in the papers that he was carrying, all went to suggest that these were men who had been alerted to his arrival in the neighbourhood and were intent on frustrating his purposes. It was not for nothing that Cutler was known as one of the sharpest of the up and coming men in the office of the District Attorney in Pharaoh and it was not long into this train of thought that he came up with the only logical and well-nigh inescapable inference that the attack tonight could only have been the work of men wishing to prevent a sheriff being appointed in Greenhaven.

When this thought struck him, he reined in and thought things over for a few minutes. Only the man heading the Greenhaven safety committee had been told of his imminent arrival. There could be no other way that those who had stopped him could possibly have known who he was or that he would be carrying any documents with him. The implications of this were disturbing in the extreme. Not least because he had gunned down two of the vigilance men from the town he was heading for. This would take some serious thinking about.

It was at this point that he was hailed from a nearby stand of trees and a sharp, authoritative voice cried out, 'Don't you move a muscle, or you're as good as dead!' It seemed that the night's adventures were not over yet.

Mark Seaton's religion was brimstone and fire Protestantism to the core, but he had always had a slight admiration for the pragmatism of the Catholic Jesuits. One maxim of that body of zealots he had particularly taken to over the years was the slogan: If the end is lawful, then the means are likewise lawful. Seaton interpreted this to mean that if you were on the right path with the Lord and doing his work, then you were pretty well justified in taking any actions in pursuit of that end. When the party of men he had despatched to intercept the District Attorney's man had returned, not only empty-handed but with one of their number stone dead, the leader of Greenhaven's vigilance committee had been reminded of this sensible saying of the Jesuits.

For over fifteen years now, Ezra Stannard had been as good a friend to Seaton as he had ever known.

Seaton had looked after Ezra's children at odd times and always helped the man as best he could in any way that he was able. If ever there was a God-fearing and pious citizen of Greenhaven, that man was Ezra Stannard. Now he was dead, gunned down like a dog on the highway and left in the dirt. Since the black-smith had been acting on his instructions, Seaton felt that the guilt for his death weighed heavily upon his own shoulders. Although none of the three men who had returned alive from the expedition had voiced the thought out loud, Seaton was sure that in their hearts, they must be blaming him for the blacksmith's untimely death and wondering what steps he would take to make things right.

As was so often the case, Seaton found that the Lord's aims and purposes happened in this case to coincide in every particular way with his own. It had taken the three surviving members of the group most of the night to get back to town. They had managed to fix up one saddle and retrieve one horse. Ezra Stannard's body had been conveyed in this way to Greenhaven, with the others trudging along wearily on foot. Tom Hanning, who had been shot, proved not to be as badly injured as at first thought and faced with the choice of being left alone out in the wild or somehow forcing himself to keep pace with his friends, chose the latter course of action.

'Any of you men read these papers?' asked Seaton when the bundle of documents was handed to him.

'Ain't hardly had the time,' remarked one of the men sourly.

Since he had confided only in Ezra Stannard the true nature of the night's business and the others had been acting as members of the safety commit-tee without knowing the facts, Seaton felt that this disaster could be easily set right; at least for the time being. After all, he was, and had been these past few decades, undertaking the Lord's work. All else was just straw in the wind set against this. It was from this perspective that Seaton, in his heart, condemned an unknown man to death. Not casually and not without considerable misgivings, but aware that in doing so he was serving the greater good of the community which he had sworn to protect from evil. 'Listen up now,' he told the men standing before him, 'There's work to be done!'

When you are certain-sure that you are doing the right thing, then there really is no limit to what steps you are liable to take in pursuit of your aims. Seaton felt both a terrible grief over the death of Ezra Stannard and a gnawing sense of his own guilt in the business. The only way to rid himself of these twin burdens was to make amends for what had happened. He couldn't bring the dead man back to life, but he could bring the killer to justice. That this would also put a stop to the plans to take from him the administration of law in those parts was, or so Seaton persuaded himself, a minor point. The main thing was to ensure that word of his role in causing the blacksmith's death did not become voiced abroad. Nothing was more calculated to damage his standing in Greenhaven and that was a thing not to be thought of. It was no longer just a question of preventing a sheriff being appointed in the town; he would never be able to hold his head up in these parts if it became known that he had needlessly caused the death of one of the best men in Greenhaven.

The sun had barely peeped over the horizon when the three men had come to see him with their tale of disaster. He would need to make his plans swiftly, working, as he was, on the reasonable assumption that this troublesome fellow might appear in town at any moment. He would have to make sure that Mr Brent Cutler didn't have the opportunity to go round stirring up discord in this peaceful town. So it was that an essentially good man turned bad, without either he himself or anybody else marking the moment. The lay preacher from the local chapel was plotting murder and truly believed in his heart that the Lord was still directing his steps.

'What would you have of me?' asked Brent Cutler, 'I'm not carrying much in the way of cash money, if that's what you're about.'

'Money?' cried the man indignantly, 'I ain't after stealing from you. It's you looks to me like you're on the scout. What d'you mean by idling your time away here in the middle o' the night? You huntin' for me or what?'

'Hunting for *you*?' said Cutler, amazed. 'I can't fathom what you're talking of. I'm not looking for anybody, just tending to my own affairs.'

'Maybe,' said the man doubtfully, 'I'll allow as you don't *sound* villainous, but a body can't be too careful.'

'You know, mister … sorry, but I didn't catch your name, I work for the District Attorney up in Pharaoh. I'm hardly likely to attack you or aught of that kind.'

'Happen you're right. Anyways, I can't carry on shouting like this, I'll make myself hoarse.' From the copse, an old man emerged. He wore no hat and both his long mane of hair and flowing beard were snow-white. He was dressed like a trapper and Cutler was strongly reminded of a couple of mountain men he'd once met. By the look of him, the fellow couldn't be a day under sixty, but Cutler would be prepared to take oath that this man could hold his own physically against somebody half his age. He looked leathery and tough, as though he lived out of doors.

Having decided that Cutler was not, after all, some wandering bandit, the old man lowered his rifle, strode up to him and thrust a hand up, saying, 'M'name's Archie. It don't signify overmuch what my other name might be; Archie'll do well enough.'

'I'm glad to know you, sir,' began Cutler, before the man cut in with the greatest irascibility, saying,

'There's no "sir" in the case, just my name'll do

well enough. We ain't in the army nor in polite society neither. What's your name, son?'

'Brent. Brent Cutler.'

'Brent it is. Well then, young Brent, are you lost or what? I was watching you some minutes from my hide over yonder and I began to suspicion you as being up to mischief. You weren't heading anywhere and looked to be waiting for something, somebody, maybe.'

'I was just thinking.'

'I'm guessing there's a story here. You want a pot of coffee?'

'You're camped out near here?'

'I live here. Come, you don't look dangerous. Don't sound so neither. I'll take a risk and let you come by my house.'

CHAPTER 4

Having decided what to do about the man from Pharaoh, Mark Seaton swung into action. He couldn't depend upon all of those in his band of vigilance men. There were those who would ask awkward questions and maybe baulk at taking the life of some official from the county seat. Well, this was one of those times when men had to be resolute in action and not spend too long debating the rights and wrongs of the case. The sooner this Brent Cutler was out of the way, the easier Seaton would feel. More to the point, the safer the town would be from the creeping corruption of the official legal system.

As a matter of fact, the methods that Seaton and his followers used were at least as effective as the official judicial system. In the last fifteen years, he and his boys had executed something over a hundred and thirty men. Of those, only two were quite innocent. In short, more than ninety-eight percent of those dealt with by the Greenhaven safety committee were guilty as sin and would have hanged just as readily had they been brought before a regular court. It was a record to be proud of. One of the two men wrongly hanged had been a half-witted drifter, who had been thought guilty of rape. The other was Brent Cutler's father.

When Seaton had seen the name Cutler on the letter from the District Attorney's office, a faint memory had stirred in his mind, but then had slipped away; elusive as a blob of quicksilver. He was sure that he had had dealings with a man of that name in the past. There was accordingly no personal animosity involved in his decision to destroy Brent Cutler; it was simply a matter of the good governance of the town.

Jack Carlton, who owned and ran the general store on Main Street, was putting up the shutters at about six that morning, when he caught sight of the leader of the vigilance men walking in his direction. He and Seaton had had good business dealings with each other in the past and Carlton knew that the head of the safety committee had a lot of respect for him. He waved and said, 'Morning there, Seaton. Goin' to be a fine day by the look of it.'

As Seaton drew closer to the storekeeper, it was clear to Jack Carlton that something was perturbing his friend's mind. 'Something I can help you with?' he asked.

'You might say so,' said Seaton. 'Ezra Stannard's been shot dead. The man that did it is still on the loose. Heading this way, maybe.'

'You don't say so?' said the other man in surprise. 'What's to do?'

The man who called himself Archie, led Cutler through the grove of trees towards a steep hillside. It wasn't until they were right upon it that what looked like a wooden hut could be discerned. It was only about six feet high and hardly as wide. Bushes grew up to the door of this structure, which meant that unless you were a few feet from it, you would never guess that there was anything to be seen. 'You live in there?' asked Cutler. 'It looks awful small.'

'Just you wait and see,' said the old man, chuckling. He directed Cutler to dismount and tether his horse on a nearby tree. When he had done this, Archie led him through the door of the hut and Cutler stopped dead in astonishment. He found himself standing in an open space as large as a fair-sized house. It was illuminated with several oil lamps, the light from which barely reached the ceiling overhead, which was lost in shadow. 'What the ...' he muttered.

'That surprised you, hey?' said the old man, cackling with pleasure.

'I don't get it,' said Cutler frankly.

'S'easy enough. This here's a cave in the side of the hill. It's limestone, goes way back. There's even a freshwater spring back a ways through another one of the caves. I just built my little shack to cover the entrance.'

'It's just fantastic. You lived here for long?'

''Bout fifteen years, I reckon. Used to live in Greenhaven, little town nigh to here.'

'Greenhaven? That's where I was headed.'

'You got business there? You ain't goin' for pleasure, I'll be bound.'

'No, you're right. It's business.'

'Well then, good luck to you. Just don't look to be having a lark there. It's a place for being sober and Godly, if that's what your tastes run to. Got three churches and every man, woman and child in that town goes to one or t'other of 'em.'

Cutler gave the old man a sharp glance. 'You don't approve of religion?'

'Religion's all well and good. I got nothing 'gainst it whatsoever. It's when folk make too much of a song an' dance about how holy and pious they are that I find it sticking in m'craw.'

'That the way of things in Greenhaven?'

The man who called himself Archie didn't reply, but walked over to what seemed to serve as a fireplace in his strange home. There were glowing embers, which he blew into life before adding a little kindling.

Cutler said, 'I'd have thought that having a fire here would smoke you out.'

'There's cracks and holes up aways, through the rock. They carry the smoke out. I'll concede that in the winter, it gets a little smoky here, though.'

'You were talking about Greenhaven,' said the

younger man, as Archie fussed about with the coffee pot. 'What sort of town is it?'

'The sort of place that I don't care to live in. I find choking on smoke at odd times is better than choking on having piety rammed down your throat all day.'

'They say that it's a peaceful town. Some folk like that.'

'It ain't often as I let anybody through my door,' remarked Archie suddenly. 'Liked the look of you, though. Seem like an honest man. You tell me what all this tends toward, meaning why you're going to Greenhaven, and then I'll think on how much I'm a goin' to say.'

It was a tricky situation. On the one hand, Brent Cutler felt disinclined to be too open and free with a man he didn't know from Adam. On the other, he had already been waylaid and robbed, presumably by men connected with Greenhaven's vigilance committee. In the end, he decided to proceed guardedly. He said, 'I'm working for the Kent County District Attorney. There are plans afoot to install a sheriff in Greenhaven.' To his annoyance, Archie burst out laughing at that; laughter which turned into a prolonged coughing fit.

'Ah Lord,' he said when he had recovered, 'you'll find that a hard row to hoe. Anybody in town got wind o' your comin'?'

'I believe my superior wrote Mr Seaton in the town,' Cutler said a little stiffly. He did not take to being laughed at like that.

'Wrote Mark Seaton, hey? How'd that go down?'

'I don't know. I left before a reply was received.'

'Listen, son,' said the old man in a fatherly way, 'I kind o' taken a liking to you. You're being cautious, which is right and proper, but suppose I tell you a bit about the town you're heading for? Just to let you know how the wind's set, so to say.'

It was while he was on the way over to see Jack Carlton that Seaton had the brilliant idea that might yet succeed in pulling all of his irons out of the fire at once. With no identification, this Cutler fellow would be mighty hard-pressed to prove he was who he said he was. Only to Ezra Stannard had he revealed some of the truth about the man from Pharaoh and now Ezra, God rest his soul, had been promoted to glory. What was to stop Seaton from portraying Brent Cutler as a ruthless and determined, murderous in fact, confidence trickster?

The more he turned this idea over in his mind, the sounder it seemed. It would be his word against Cutler's and after the death of such a well-beloved local man as Ezra, nobody would be likely to listen too much to anything the killer had to say in his defence. It would sound like the ravings of a lunatic. With luck, they could have the man disposed of in next to no time and after that, well they'd just have to wait and see.

So it was that when Carlton asked what was on his

mind that fine morning, he was able to tell him quite truthfully that Ezra Stannard had been killed while undertaking his duty as a vigilance man. As he was out-lining the matter to Carlton and explaining the need to raise a large posse and track the killer down, a man came looking for him with the news that Tom Hanning's wound had proved worse than anybody had realized. He had suffered some kind of seizure not half an hour since, which had been quickly followed by his death. Saddened as Seaton was by another death, it was not difficult to see that two deaths like this would serve to rouse everybody in Greenhaven and ensure that when he was caught, the man from the District Attorney's office would get short shrift. With good fortune, the whole affair might be wrapped up by nightfall.

'Men don't change their natures,' said Archie, as he poured out a cup of coffee, 'not just 'cause o' what some preacher man says. They might hide what they're up to, from shame, but they're goin' to carry on acting the same way.'

After the two of them were seated on the sur-prisingly comfortable chairs that the old man had fashioned himself from the trees growing thereabouts, he continued.

'Greenhaven used to be as rough as all get out. Early years o' the war, well it was like nothing you ever dreamed of. Guns, liquor, women and I don't know what-all else. Every comanchero, moonshiner and bandit for miles around made their homes nigh to the town. Men's daughters and wives weren't safe on the streets in broad daylight. I tell you, it was a plain scandal the way things got.'

'But it's not like that any more, is that right?'

'Not since a fellow called Mark Seaton took charge of what they call the safety committee, no. Town's as quiet as you like these days.'

'So what's wrong with that?' asked Cutler. 'I don't get why folk wouldn't be pleased.'

'Like I said, you can hide some things, but you can't get rid of 'em. All that's happened is that all the crime and so on has moved out of the town itself. You can still get a woman or buy stolen goods, only now you need to go a mile or two out of town, to some farmhouse. But there's worse than that. It ain't just the hypocrisy. More than one of them in Seaton's blamed vigilance committee are up to all sorts of villainy themselves, but he doesn't notice. Long as a man goes to church on the Sabbath and refrains from swearing and blaspheming in his presence, Seaton thinks he's good and righteous. Huh! One or two of those boys who keep order in Greenhaven are worse than any bushwhacker.'

'And Seaton doesn't know about it?'

Archie chuckled. 'Not he. Like I say, with him it's all outward appearance. Long as men behave right and say their prayers, he thinks they're fine fellows. I tell you now, there's things go on out of sight of the town which wouldn't be tolerated if they were known of.'

At this, Cutler's ears pricked up and he asked, 'What sort of things, sir?'

'Archie. M'name's Archie. Well, slavin' for one.'

'Slaving? You're not serious. You don't mean here in this territory? Who's doing it?'

'Mexicans, chiefly. Agents up north get young girls to come down this way. Promise 'em all sort of foolishness. Jobs in theatres, dancing, all manner of things. When they get down here, they're like then to fetch up working in some hurdy-gurdy house. If not, they end up with a bunch of comancheros who somehow spirit them across the border. They end up in cathouses all over Mexico.'

Brent Cutler was ashen with horror. He had never heard anything so appalling in his life. He said, 'You're certain-sure about this? It's not just rumour or wild stories?'

'Not a bit of it,' replied Archie, hugely satisfied with the effect that he observed his news had had on the youngster. 'They don't all know of it in Greenhaven, but then they don't *want* to know of such things. Long as the streets are safe for their own womenfolk, why should they care?'

'You say the safety committee or whatever they call it there, some of them are in this racket?'

'One or two of 'em, sure. Other things too. It's what I said, you can hide men's base instincts, keep 'em out of the way, but you ain't a going to do away with them. Not no how.'

'Do many people hereabouts know of this?'

'They don't *want* to know. Why rock the boat? Once in a while, somebody comes sniffing round, but outsiders don't generally find out much. There's accidents; one fell down an old mine shaft; one fellow even got strung up by the vigilance men themselves. Can you believe it? Yes sir, they hanged a US marshal.'

A strange feeling came over Cutler, as though somebody had walked over his grave. He could feel gooseflesh puckering up the skin on his arms and said casually, 'Hanged a lawman? That makes strange listening. What happened?'

'It was the damnedest thing. Must have been ten, maybe twelve years ago. Some fellow came down here, only a few years after Mark Seaton took charge of the vigilance men. I was still spending a lot of time in town in those days and soon as I set eyes on that man I said to myself, he's a lawman or I'm a Dutchman. There was some lively games going on at that time, year or two after the war ended it would have been. Anyway, a stage was knocked over, few miles from here. Up by the High Peaks. Somehow the word was out that this fellow was in on it.'

'I suppose you can't – I know it was a while back – you can't recollect his name, I guess?'

Old Archie looked at him queerly and said slowly, 'That I can't, son. Not after all these years. Anyways, Seaton and a few of his boys they chased him miles. Tracked him down to a little town and then hanged

him on the spot. Word was they found some com-
promising evidence as clinched the case 'gainst him.
There was the hell of a row, though, 'cause they did
this in somebody else's town and the local people
weren't none too pleased 'bout it.'

'Any idea what town that was?'

'I couldn't say. I mind that there was a landing or
some such in the name of it. More than that, I couldn't
be sure.'

'It wouldn't have been Grant's Landing by some
chance?'

'Grant's Landing! That's it, for a bet. Why, I ain't
thought on that these ten years or more. Yes, it was
Grant's Landing. But how come you'd be knowing
that?'

Brent Cutler shook his head; his heart was too full
to speak. All these years he had known full well that
his father hadn't been any sort of criminal. He'd
known it, but hadn't had a speck of evidence to back
up his belief. They'd moved on almost immediately
after the death of his father and anybody wishing to
track them down wouldn't have had an easy time of it.
So terrible had been the fear of something happening
to her children after the lynching of her husband, that
his mother had wanted to make tracks at once, not
even delaying for a funeral.

Archie was looking at the young man thoughtfully,
as though he might be on the verge of saying something further. Then he apparently decided against

it, saying merely, 'You want to sleep on the floor here tonight, then be my guest.'

There were currently three members of the Greenhaven safety committee who, in addition to their regular employment in the town, moved on the fringes of various criminal enterprises. Two of these men didn't make anything like a fortune from their crooked activities; they merely received payment from some of those running various enterprises around Greenhaven and some additional money for providing warning of what was planned and misleading the rest of the safety committee about this and that, as occasion demanded. The men they tipped off were moonshiners and similar small fry. The third of the men was a horse of another colour; making a good deal of money from his activities beyond the law. This man was Jack Carlton, who the leader of the Greenhaven vigilance men regarded as his most stalwart lieutenant.

Most of the crime which took place in the vicinity of the town was run-of-the-mill stuff such as drinking dens, the unregulated buying and selling of gold, a little gun-running to the Indians and so on. Sometimes there was more seriously illegal activity – holding up of stages and so on. In recent years there had also been, as Brent Cutler had lately learned, a growing number of white slavers operating in the area. Now of all crimes, none was viewed with more loathing and detestation by the average citizen than the trafficking of white women.

There was always a demand for attractive girls in the hurdy-gurdy houses, saloons and musical theatres of the rougher towns, especially those where, for one reason or another, men had plenty of money to splash around. In the wake of gold rushes, such places sprung up like mushrooms. In some of these establishments, prostitution was so rife that there was little to distinguish them from cathouses. All this was dreadful enough, with innocent and inexperienced girls being lured from remote farms on the promise of making their fortune in the theatre. There was worse, though, and that was the transferring of women across the border into Mexico, where they were virtually held prisoner and forced to work in brothels. Anybody detected in this vile trade was pretty well certain to be lynched on the spot; even in districts which boasted a sheriff and properly constituted courts.

With Greenhaven being less than a hundred miles from the border, it might reasonably have been expected that the town would be used as a staging post for the activities of the white slavers, as indeed it had been before Mark Seaton set up his safety committee. Having such a fierce and righteous man heading the vigilance men there these days, meant that even visiting Greenhaven to stock up on food or to buy powder and liquor was apt to be a hazardous undertaking. The least suspicion that a man might even be consorting with those transporting women into Mexico could be enough to put his neck in jeopardy.

All of which provided a lucrative business opportunity for Jack Carlton, who kept the general store in Greenhaven. The men who escorted the women south towards the border, comancheros in the main, were seldom welcomed in respectable towns. This was particularly so in Greenhaven, where anything which even hinted at criminality was frowned upon and vigorously discouraged in the most practical way possible. Carlton drove wagons of provisions out to the comancheros where they were camped out in the hills. The wagons were often loaded not only with food and liquor, but also firearms, powder and shot as required. This enabled Carlton to profit in two ways. Firstly, by the enormous mark-up he applied to any such goods taken to the slavers and secondly by taking a regular payment from the men in order to help them chart a course through the territory which would enable them to avoid trouble en route.

Because the leader of the Greenhaven vigilance men was known to be such a sea-green incorruptible, towns for miles around shared information with him about any strange goings on in their own areas. He in turned confided in Jack Carlton and Ezra Stannard, which meant that those two men knew to the most exact measure which districts it might be wise for the comanchero bands and their wagon trains to steer clear of.

Stannard, who had so recently departed this life,

was as honest as the day is long, but Carlton was something else again. He was no fool and allowed himself no outward show of the wealth which he had been steadily accumulating since settling in Greenhaven five years earlier. To all appearances, he was no more than a moderately successful storekeeper who made a reasonable living at his trade and resided quietly in town, attending chapel and so on. It was his belief that in another year or two, he would have amassed enough to move away from Greenhaven and be able to live on the proceeds of his dealings with the slavers.

Like Mark Seaton, although of course for very different reasons, Carlton was very anxious not to see a sheriff taking charge in the town. It would altogether queer his pitch. Before he had set off the previous night, Ezra Stannard, that simple and trusting soul, had shared with Carlton the motive for bushwhacking this Brent Cutler and turning him loose without his clothing. So it was that when Seaton came to him that morning with this cock and bull story about some confidence man who had, while Stannard and a few others had been in the process of scaring him off, killed two of them, Jack Carlton listened carefully and decided that there was no percentage in telling Seaton that his story was all a pail of hogwash. Instead, he asked, 'You want that we should take this Cutler fellow and hang him for murder? That's only just, after what he's done.'

'I knew you'd see it so,' said Seaton, visibly relieved. 'Only thing is, this man is like to spin a heap of foolish stories to save his neck.'

'You don't say so?' replied Jack Carlton, in apparent surprise. 'What sort of stories might he try and sell us?'

CHAPTER 5

When he woke the next morning, Cutler couldn't for a moment recall where he might be. The events of the previous night were vague and distorted and for a short time, he wondered if he had perhaps dreamed some of what had happened. The fact that he found himself on waking in a gloomy cave with the only light streaming in through the open door of the shack built over the mouth of the cave served to reassure him, however. If he hadn't dreamed about the old man living in a cave, then like as not the rest of what he thought had befallen him was also veridical.

At first, the most vivid and alarming of his recollections was the fact that he had killed a man only a few hours since. Then he remembered what he had been told of the lawman being lynched at Grant's Landing and he felt as though somebody had punched him in the belly. Although he'd been only a child at the time, hearing his father cry that he was a peace officer was as fresh in his memory as though it happened only that day.

The death of his father had been a mystery for all his youth. His mother knew nothing about her husband's affairs and neither did her parents. It seemed to be a toss-up as to whether folk believed that his pa had been a bandit or the victim of mistaken identification. He had never heard the serious proposition advanced that there was any more than that to be said. After all, he alone had heard that despairing shout: 'I'm a peace officer!'

The light from the doorway dimmed momentarily as it was blocked by somebody entering the cave. The man he knew as Archie said, 'Ah, you're back with us, are you? Thought you was going to slumber the whole day through.'

'What time is it?'

'I ain't got no pocket watch, nor clock neither. I'd say it's about nine.'

Cutler sat up and stretched. He said, 'I'm much obliged to you for your offer of shelter last night. I'd best be off now. Thank you again.'

'Well now, what's your hurry, boy? There's one or two things doing as you might wish to know of. You said last night that you're some kind of law. That true?'

'It's true that I work for the District Attorney, yes. I don't know that that makes me any sort of "law", though. I've no powers of arrest or anything.'

'That don't signify. You got a gun, ain't you?'

'You must forgive me, Mr— Archie. I don't know that I'm properly awake yet. Could you tell me what this is all about?'

'Young people is soft today. Don't rise till the day's half done and even then they're sleepy and stupid. I reckon you'll need some vittles in you and mayhap a pot o' coffee 'fore you're able to function?'

'A bite to eat and some coffee would be welcome enough, that's true.'

At about the same time that the young man from Pharaoh was breaking his fast up in the area between Fort James and Greenhaven, Jack Carlton was setting out with a buckboard loaded with a dozen rifles and a keg of powder. Another of his sidelines was buying outdated weapons dirt cheap and then selling them on to men who would in turn run them into the Indian Nations. There was enough money in this business for both Carlton and the men he traded with to make a decent profit out it. The rifles were former army stock; muzzle-loaders from the war. Antiquated as they were, the Indians were always in the market for firearms, which they could not legally acquire themselves. As he was already heading towards Fort James on this little piece of business, it would be convenient too to drop by and visit with a group of comancheros who were waiting for some women being escorted south.

Before parting that morning, Mark Seaton had said, 'This Cutler fellow might fetch up at any moment.

We have to make sure that he doesn't have a chance to start spreading his lies and confusing folk, you understand what I'm saying?'

'Sure,' Carlton had said equably. 'There might be those who'd give credence to what this trickster might be saying. That wouldn't do.'

Seaton had shot him a sharp, sidelong glance at that, almost as though he thought that the other man might be making game of him; as was indeed the case. To smooth things over, Carlton said, 'I've got deliveries to make to one or two little places up towards Fort James. From what you say, this fellow might be heading this way from that direction. I'll be sure to set watch for him.'

'That's the ticket. What time do you reckon to get back here?'

'Oh, I should be back by mid-afternoon. Then we can take counsel with some of the others and carry out a search for this scamp.'

So the two of them had parted amicably, with Seaton entertaining not the least suspicion of the man who he saw as a close and valued comrade. For his own part, Carlton was lost in admiration for the head of the safety committee. Seldom had he heard a man lie so fluently and with such confidence. It was a novel experience to learn that the starchy preacher was as capable as the next man of deceiving his neighbours.

Disposing of the muskets took no time at all, as the price had been arranged beforehand, which meant there was no dickering. When the money and goods had changed hands, Carlton and the men who had come for the guns took time to light their pipes and shoot the breeze for a spell. Casually, Carlton said, 'Hear anything of some plan to bring in sheriffs hereabouts?'

Touching as it did upon their professional lives, this was a topic dear to the hearts of the gun-runners. One of them said, 'You talkin' o' that bastard up in Pharaoh?'

'The District Attorney? Yeah, maybe I am. Know anything about it?'

One of the men spat in the dirt and said, 'It's that damned governor, him being so all-fired keen to join the Union. It's him as is makin' the running.'

'Anything happening in that direction over at Fort James?' asked Carlton.

'That place?' the man laughed. ''Nother year and it'll be a ghost town there. No, I guess you'd have to look a bit closer to home. They say it's towns above five hundred souls that they're looking at just now.'

The man's companion, an unkempt and ill-favoured half-breed, said, 'Same like I heard. How many people you got up at Greenhaven these days?'

After they'd eaten, Archie said, 'If you're the law, then I guess you'll be wantin' to help me tonight. It bein', as you might say, in the law enforcement field.'

'What do you mean?' asked Brent Cutler curiously.

'It's like this, son,' said the old man, 'the citizens of Greenhaven are happy enough, long as their own town is clean and safe. Not that I blame 'em. Me, I like a drink, game of cards and suchlike. One thing I can't abide, though, is men mistreating women.'

'Me neither,' said Cutler, unsure where the conversation was tending.

'Well, I said that there's slavin' goes on near here at odd times. Men bringing women who've been promised jobs, you follow me?'

'Sure.'

'Well, those as get this far ain't gettin' jobs in hurdy-gurdys. They're bein' taken into Mexico.'

'It's a filthy business.'

'Thought you'd say so,' said Archie. 'Well, odd times, I taken it upon my own self to stop some o' them boys in their tracks. Some I shoots; others I set their wagons and other gear afire. It all goes to putting a stop to those goings on. There's a bunch o' them vermin camped out, not three miles from here. Word is they're waiting for a consignment of girls, then they're a goin' to make tracks for the Rio Grande.'

'I work in an office. I don't know that I could get mixed up in such a thing. It wouldn't look good. Still and all, if nobody's doing anything about it—'

'You want in?'

'Yes, you can count me in. There's something of a problem come up with my regular work anyway. I need to think about it before I proceed further. But I tell you now, I haven't had a heap of experience with weapons or anything. I might turn out to be more of a hindrance than a help to you.'

'I should think there's more to you than meets the eye, boy.'

The plan, as the old man set it out, was that they should take some oil and do as much damage as they could to the wagons and other equipment where the comancheros were established. They seemingly went off for hours at a time, leaving their camp untended. If enough havoc could be wrought, then it was just possible that they would not be able to move the girls across the border.

'How are they transporting these young women?' asked Cutler. 'They keep them hog-tied or what? Otherwise, why don't they try and run for it?'

'Poor fools don't know what they're heading for. They've had their heads stuffed with a lot of nonsense about acting and dancing. Think that they'll be the admiration of some city in this country. They're plumb ignorant, most of 'em. Come from as far away as Montana and Wyoming. Why, they don't even know half the time that they've crossed into Mexico. I've heard some terrible stories about it. Some of them aren't above fourteen, fifteen years of age.

'I don't know but what,' said Cutler slowly, 'that I haven't a duty to tackle crimes such as that. I've been sent down here to help establish the rule of law and if that means anything, it must mean protecting the innocent. If I can be any use to you, then I'll surely take a hand in it.'

Jack Carlton very nearly didn't make it to the comancheros' base. After parting from the men to whom he'd sold the rifles, he set off into the hills at a leisurely trot. The buckboard was rattling along and he was in no particular hurry. When a bullet went droning past his head like an angry hornet, it gave him the shock of his life. He halted the wagon at once, looking round to see where the man who had shot at him might be concealed. He was tempted to reach out from the back of the buckboard his own rifle – the latest model Winchester. The only thing that stopped him doing so was the apprehension that it might cause the unseen gunman to take another shot at him. Instead, he sat patiently and waited to see what would happen next. At the forefront of his mind was the fear that the next development might be another bullet; one sent straight through his heart or head.

As it was, a young man, who had seemingly been crouching in the shrubbery covering the approach to the hills, stood up; his rifle was still at his shoulder and pointing straight at Carlton. He was about fifty yards away.

'What you want?' called the youth, in a strong Spanish accent.

'I've come to see them as is camped up in the little valley yonder,' called back Jack Carlton. 'They know me well enough. Ask a chap by the name of Alfred.'

'You stay. Don't move none!' shouted back the boy. He approached cautiously, keeping his rifle trained on Carlton as he came on. This proceeding made Carlton exceedingly uncomfortable, it needing only for the boy to stub his toe and he might end up firing accidentally. When he was only six feet away from the buckboard, the young man halted and said, 'I get up. Ride with you, make sure no lies.'

'Sure,' replied Carlton pleasantly, 'up you get.' He extended his hand, as though to help haul up the man. Instinctively, the Mexican stretched out his own hand, lowering his weapon as he did so. As soon as he had the youth's hand in his, Carlton gripped it tight to stop him from withdrawing it. Then he twisted the fellow's wrist sharply and launched himself off the buckboard, sending the two of them rolling in the dirt. The rifle went flying out of reach and the Mexican's hand snaked down to the pistol at his hip. 'Oh no you don't, you son of a bitch!' exclaimed Carlton, grabbing the pistol and flinging it out of reach. Then he gave the younger man a ferocious and methodical beating. By the time he was finished, his own knuckles were grazed and he was a little out of breath. The man who had accosted him, however, was lying on the grass helplessly, groaning in agony. There was blood all over his face from a hefty blow which Carlton had delivered to his nose.

Carlton stood up and said quietly, 'Next time you

see me coming, don't you fire at me. I won't have it. And don't go pointing guns at me, neither. Makes me nervous.' Then he climbed back onto the buckboard, touched up the horse and continued his journey.

Mark Seaton was feeling increasingly confident of his ability to get the genie back into the bottle. During the course of the day, he went by several businesses and alerted the owners to the fact that he wished to put together a posse to hunt down the ruthless killer who had done for Ezra Stannard and Tom Hanning. There was widespread anger about the murders and he hadn't anticipated any problem about raising enough men for the task. With a little good fortune, the fellow from Pharaoh would start shooting when he found that he was about to be apprehended. All things considered, this would be the neatest solution by far. Seaton didn't really think it likely that any of the men would set a great store by the ramblings of a killer, but better by far that this Cutler wasn't even given the chance to cause doubt and sow uncertainty in anybody's mind.

While he was making his rounds on this duty, Seaton dropped by the *Lucky Man*, with the aim of having a quiet word in the owner's ear. One of the things that most exercised the mind of the self-appointed superintendent of the town's morals was the question of hard liquor and the ill effects it brought about. Although he was a strict temperance man himself, Seaton had no objection to other, weaker souls enjoying a draught of porter or even a shot of whiskey from time to time. However, as long as he was in charge of the matter, he made sure that the saloons closed at a Godly hour and didn't open at all on the Sabbath. This was irksome to the owners of Greenhaven's two bars, because they knew very well that if they closed promptly at ten in the evening, as Seaton insisted, then their patrons would ride off to one of the drinking places which existed a mile or two from town. These were really no more than barns with a few benches, which served poteen, but it was money taken from the saloon owners' pockets when they turned away customers like that and so they often tried to extend their opening hours a little.

At about the same time that Jack Carlton was arriving at the camp of the comancheros and Mark Seaton was berating the barkeep at the *Lucky Man* for serving folk after hours, Cutler was helping the old man called Archie to rig up what was essentially a fire bomb.

Of course, thought Cutler as he worked, it could be that this man is some old rogue using me as a cat's paw for purposes of his own. He glanced sideways at the man next to him and was instantly reassured. Whatever else Archie was, he was no villain. Cutler had already heard about the forcing into prostitution of young women and girls before he'd met Archie. It was one of those things that the governor was keen to suppress before he officially applied for statehood for the territory; slave trading being one of those activities apt to make a district seem backwards and primitive. There had been rumours in the District Attorney's office that the governor was considering the use of troops to put a stop to the tricks of the comancheros. If he, Cutler, could throw a wrench in the works of such men, he was happy enough to do so. It might not do his career any harm in the future either, acquiring a little firsthand experience of the white slavers.

'You dreaming, boy?' said the old man irritably, 'I asked you twice for that hammer.'

'Sorry. I was miles away.' He handed the hammer to Archie, who banged a few tacks into the keg upon which he was working.

The device they were constructing was simplicity itself. It consisted of a wooden barrel, about two feet long, with clay pots securely lashed with wire to both ends. The keg would be half filled with lamp oil before use. The clay pots were each stuffed with gunpowder and bits of scrap iron such as rusty nails. According to Archie, the men who were waiting for the next group of girls were camped out in the hills. They generally stayed in a little hollow, which sheltered them from the wind. The important thing of note about this location was that the walls of the hollow were like a saucer-shaped depression at the bottom before rising more steeply up to the surrounding hills.

What the old man had in mind was to creep up to the top of the slopes and then light a fuse attached to the keg. This would then be sent rolling down to where the wagons, carts and supplies of the comancheros lay at the bottom. The lamp oil would set everything alight, with luck, and when the flames reached the improvised mines with their deadly charge, these would explode like artillery shells.

'If that don't spike their guns, I'm a Dutchman!' the old man had declared.

It was a while since Cutler had done any work of this sort with his hands and he did not find the experience at all displeasing. He spent so much of his time lately shuffling papers about in an office, that he had all but forgotten the pleasure of creating something in this way.

At length, they were finished and the two of them sat there, looking at their deadly creation. 'Well,' said Archie, 'if that don't settle 'em, then I'm sure I don't know what will. Come nightfall, if you're still game, we'll cart that up to their blamed camp and see if we can't show them as they ain't welcome in these here parts.'

'I'm game,' said Cutler quietly.

CHAPTER 6

Some of the comancheros, who were primarily based in New Mexico and Texas, were no more than traders who bartered cloth, tools, bread and guns with the Kiowa and Comanche, receiving in exchange hides, ponies and sometimes slaves. Others lived a nomadic life of banditry, preying upon lonely homesteads and robbing travellers. There were also those, like the bands who passed through the territory on the way to Mexico, who transported women from place to place. It was seldom that only one group was involved in such transactions. The various factions tended to keep to one area and would sell on commodities to each other, be those commodities ponies, beaver pelts or young girls. In the present instance, one group of men was escorting the party of girls south, from just across the line where the territory began, and they would then hand them over, for a consideration, to the bunch now waiting in the hills up towards Fort James. These boys would then take their cargo south, eventually crossing the Rio Grande into Mexico.

There were eighteen men camped out, waiting for the girls to arrive. They understood that there would be eleven girls to escort south, ranging in age from fourteen upwards. The profits to be made in Chihuahua from a dozen young, Anglo virgins was likely to be stupendous. True, there was some initial outlay, but even so, they would none of them be short of cash money for the foreseeable future after delivering these girls to the brothel keepers who had already contracted to purchase them.

Although they didn't apprehend any danger from the local vigilance men, the comancheros were taking no chances, which is why Jack Carlton had received a warning shot across his bows as he approached the temporary base. His arrival, after the little bit of friction with the young man acting as lookout, was greeted with unbounded enthusiasm. Eighteen men need a good deal of food and drink and being sequestered up there, in the foothills of the High Peaks, meant that they were more or less reliant on what Carlton brought up in his buckboard. He hadn't been able to come for four days and they were accordingly on short commons.

'Ai, you bastard!' cried one of the men, when Carlton's rattling wagon hove into view. 'What kept you?'

'Would o' been here sooner, but for some boy shooting at me just now.'

'Well, praise God, you're here now. What have you for us?'

The buckboard was swiftly divested of its contents, for all of which, Jack Carlton had been shrewd enough to obtain payment in advance. Truth to tell, he would be sorry to see the back of these boys when they moved on the next day. Their custom always provided him with a welcome boost in his financial resources. The mark-up on the goods he sold them was a considerable one.

'What word from your vigilantes?' asked one of the men.

'Nothing to concern you, although a posse might be riding out in this direction tonight. They ain't lookin' for you boys, though.'

'They coming up in the hills?'

'No reason why they would. We're looking for a fellow as shot dead two of our men.'

'You'll be riding with them?' asked another of the men.

'Yes, yes,' replied Carlton impatiently. 'Don't fret, it'll be fine. Just keep your heads down and don't show your faces after dark. And I wouldn't let that young fool that shot at me go out on the rampage. Anybody shoots at that posse and there'll be hell to pay.'

This was another of the services that Carlton provided, and was paid for. He was in a good position to lead the vigilance men off on a snipe hunt when circumstances required.

Having delivered the goods, there was little point in lingering further. Carlton had no particular liking for these rogues and knew that they would cheerfully cut his throat if they thought that there was any advantage to themselves in doing so. They had only refrained so far because he was so useful to them. 'It's been good to visit with you folks,' said Carlton, 'but I guess I'd best be getting along now.' There were a few grunts, but none of them were really all that interested in his departure. He manoeuvred his horse carefully around the heaps of saddlery, boxes and other gear that was stowed around the three carts in which the women were to be travelling. As he left, it struck Carlton that the comanchero camp bore some little resemblance to a travelling circus.

While his chief deputy was betraying him up by the High Peaks, Mark Seaton was putting together a posse to ride out later that evening in an effort to track down and hang Brent Cutler. Practically every adult man in Greenhaven contributed a dollar a month to the safety committee. This was then used to pay the expenses of those who abandoned their work while riding in pursuit of wrongdoers. It was a simple enough system, but had worked smoothly for the better part of twenty years. There was no bureaucracy involved, no paperwork and no tiresome waits for justice to be delivered. For all the irritation of not being able to get a drink after ten at night and having to ride off on a six mile round trip to have a whore, most all the townsfolk thought that they were getting good value for their money. It was truly said that a child of tender years or a lone young woman could have walked down the meanest alley in Greenhaven at any hour of the day or night, without the least fear of being troubled or interfered with in any way.

The first person Seaton called on was James Booker, who owned some of the pastures which surrounded the town. Booker greeted him affably and had already guessed the reason for the visit. 'This'll be about that devil as shot Ezra Stannard? Count me in.'

The others Seaton called upon that day were similarly ready to do their duty. The blacksmith had been a popular figure locally and his murder had excited great disgust and a burning desire for retribution upon the sort of person who could casually snuff out the life of such a good man. As he went on his rounds, Seaton made sure to emphasize the fact that the fellow they were hunting for was a silver-tongued liar, who made his crooked living by spinning plausible stories to the widow and orphan; cheating them of their money in this way. By the time he had finished, there wasn't a one of the posse who would have given the slightest credence to anything that Cutler tried to tell them.

Knowing that Cutler genuinely was coming to town as a representative of the District Attorney's office in Pharaoh gave Seaton an edge in predicting the man's movements. If he really had been some random confidence man, on the roam and looking for an easy mark, then the encounter with four men from Greenhaven would have spooked him and he would most likely have been halfway across the territory by now. Since this Cutler knew that he was in the right, he would, on the other hand, probably see no reason to alter his course. He was in all probability still heading towards Greenhaven. Fact was, Seaton had expected him to arrive before this and the delay gave him cause to hope that the fellow had met an unfortunate accident somewhere on the road; for preference, a lethal one.

By two that afternoon, ten men had positively engaged to ride out at dusk to seek for this scoundrel. It would be a relief to Seaton when Carlton returned from his business. Now that Ezra Stannard was gone, the owner of the store was the most reliable and trustworthy of the safety committee and Seaton would be glad to have the man at his side when they rode out that night.

After finishing off the strange device whose construction the man called Archie had directed, the two of them went back and sat outside the old man's cave home and had a bite to eat. 'How do you get by for food?' inquired Cutler curiously.

'I hunt and trap. Visit town when I want somethin' in particular.'

'What about money?'

Archie shot the other a sharp look and said, 'Ah, you're the genuine article all right. Trust a lawyer to ask so much o' questions. It's no secret. I do some prospecting up in the streams near here. There's enough placer for me to live on. I get by.'

'I didn't mean to be inquisitive. It's just that with such a comfortable life, I'm surprised you want to start a range war with those comancheros.'

'Some things I can't abide,' said Archie shortly. 'One of 'em's pushing around the weak and helpless. I can put up with a thief, even tolerate a killer. I won't have this vile trade going on right on my very doorstep, so to speak.'

'I wonder you don't just move to Greenhaven and join the vigilance men there.'

The old man burst out laughing at that. 'What, and start fretting 'cause a man wants a drink on the Sabbath or is buying and selling guns to those he oughtn't? I got no time for that sort of foolishness. Forcing girls who're no more than children into a whorehouse, that's something else again.'

It seemed to Cutler that it would do no harm at all to delay his arrival in Greenhaven by a day or two. If his suspicions were correct and the man he had shot dead had indeed been a member of their vigilance committee, then it made sense to give a little time for feelings to cool. At the moment, it was altogether possible that some of those in the town might be a little ticked off with him. The fact that he also lacked his letters of authority and so on was also something to weigh in the balance when considering how to turn up in Greenhaven. Obviously, Mark Seaton would know of his coming, but then again, it could well have been this very man who had sent out four emissaries to greet him in such a discouraging fashion. This would need a lot of thinking and in the meantime, there were certainly worse ways of biding his time than by helping this good man to tackle a gang of slavers.

'What time should we set off?' asked Cutler.

'I reckon their friends'll be coming just about sundown,' said Archie. 'They'll hand over the girls to the scamps who're camped near here and then the other group'll head back north again. From what I know of 'em, they'll make the exchange out on the plain, before the hills start. That will be our best time.'

'You taken action of this sort before?'

'Not precisely like this. I done stuff that slowed them down, muddled them up. Those boys don't seem able to take a hint, though. I'm hopin' as this'll give them a message they'll take heed of for a good long while.'

As he drove his cart back to Greenhaven, Jack Carlton mulled over in his mind whether there was some way that he could make capital from his knowledge of Seaton's duplicity. It was fairly plain that the leader of the safety committee wouldn't be overly keen on some outsider breezing in and taking over law enforcement in the town. Simply knowing that Seaton had told a barefaced lie about this business to Carlton, told that individual all that he needed to know. The question was, could he turn this to his advantage? It was mighty dull being Seaton's friend, no matter how much good stead this stood him in, in the eyes of the town. He was trusted far more as a close confederate of the Godly Mark Seaton than ever he would have been on his own merits.

By the time he was back on the outskirts of Greenhaven, Carlton's schemes had solidified into the blackmailing of the town's leading citizen. It would take a little doing and once he tipped his hand, Seaton would know that his supposed friend was anything but; on the whole, though, the profits of such a move would vastly outweigh any such minor disadvantages. There would be no purpose in making a move until they had run down and destroyed this man from Pharaoh, of whose swift death Jack Carlton was every bit as desirous as Seaton was himself. It was in nobody's interests to have strangers sniffing around Greenhaven and its environs; least of all strangers from the District Attorney's office!

It was a relief to Seaton to spot his friend ambling back along Main Street with that old buckboard of his. He hailed the storekeeper at once, crying good-naturedly, 'You surely took your time, Jack. What kept you?'

'Ah, you know what it's like. People counting out the

money they owe me in nickels and dimes. Who'd be in business, hey?'

'You ready for tonight?'

'Why, yes. You think this fellow is still likely to be in the vicinity?'

'I see no harm in looking for him, that's for sure.'

'Happen you're right. What time you want to ride, about six or seven?'

'I thought seven, if that accords with your convenience?'

'I reckon so. Gives me time to deal with one or two little matters. Where do we muster, edge of town?'

'Yes. I've told the others to meet at the livery stable.'

'I'll see you there.'

The sun crept slowly around the sky; falling until it touched the western horizon. All except two of the comancheros left the camp to collect the girls whom they were awaiting. These men, so ready to betray or double cross others, lived in constant fear of the same happening to them. They wanted to make sure that if there were to be any species of violence with the other band arriving in the area, that there would be enough of them to give good account of themselves. The two who remained in camp were the young man who Jack Carlton had beaten earlier that day and another boy, who was only sixteen. Their instructions were merely to set a watch upon the carts and so on and to see that no harm befell any of the belongings of the other men.

Although he hadn't known it at the time he acted, the boy who Carlton had beaten up was the near relative of one of the older men at the camp. Luckily for Carlton, this comanchero had been away and not returned until after Carlton had gone back to Greenhaven. When he saw the state of his sister's son, this man had sworn that if ever his path crossed with that of Jack Carlton again, then it would be Carlton's face which was left bloody and bruised.

The two youngsters, not expecting any sort of problem, fell to fooling around chatting about inconsequential matters. Had they be doing as they had been instructed and looking round and listening for trouble, then they might just possibly have heard the two men who had scrambled up the other side of one of the slopes leading down to the comanchero camp. They had made a not inconsiderable amount of noise in doing so, for they not only had to haul their own selves up the scree-strewn slope; they were also encumbered by a heavy and awkward burden, which had to be dragged up by ropes.

When Cutler and Archie gained the top of the slope, they lay for a moment, pulling on the ropes and slowly dragging up the wooden keg. They were morbidly aware of the noise that this generated, as stones went skittering down the slope, but there were no sounds of alarm from the camp on the other side of the ridge. 'Think they've heard anything?' whispered Cutler.

'Wouldn't o' thought so. Those hoof beats we heard earlier sounded to me like the whole boilin' of 'em's most likely left. I'll have a peek over yonder and see what's what.' Archie crawled up to the top of the slope and cautiously peered over into the little valley below. He came back and said, 'Couldn't be better. There's two boys been left in charge. They're having a wrestlin' match right now.'

Now that it had come to the point, Cutler was gripped with a sudden uncertainty about the course of action that he and Archie were about to embark upon. He said, 'You're sure about this?'

'I'll do it all by my own self, if you'd rather.'

'No, I guess I'm in it now.'

The two of them carefully heaved their homemade bomb up to the top of the slope. The wagons below were only two hundred yards or so away. 'Let's do it, then!' said Cutler.

Archie took out an old-fashioned tinder box and struck the steel, setting sparks into a little wad of dried moss. He had to do this three times before it caught flame. Then he applied the fire to the fuse, which had already been attached to the barrel. It sputtered and then began burning fiercely. He said, 'On the count of three, boy. One, two, three!'

They both gave the device a shove, which sent it over the rim of the slope.

Incredible to relate, the two lookouts at the camp had still not noticed anything amiss. They were now sitting with their backs to Cutler and Archie. Cutler said anxiously, 'I hope they get out of the way.'

'It's all the same to me if they don't,' said his companion indifferently. 'They know what's afoot, same as the rest of them. You make your bed hard and lie on it.'

While Archie was talking, Cutler watched as the rolling keg slowly picked up speed and began to career down the rocky slope, heading straight for the wagons. It was throwing off sparks and was now clearly audible as it scattered stones and dirt in its wake. At last, one of the young men slouching against a wagon turned round to see what was causing the noise. He leaped up in alarm when he saw the cause, tugging at his companion's arm to alert him too to his peril. They both ran from the spot where the barrel looked likely to strike.

The effect of their stratagem was all that Archie and his young assistant could have hoped for. When it smashed into the wagon, the keg split open, spilling lamp oil in all directions. Almost immediately this ignited, throwing up a sheet of smoky flames. The young men had no idea at all how to deal with this crisis. They ran back and forth shouting and swearing, before one of them thought to fetch some water. By this time, two of the wagons were covered in burning oil and the sensible dodge would have been to manhandle the third cart to safety. This evidently did not occur to either of them. It was when the older of the two boys went over to the blazing wagons with a bucket of water that the first of the jars packed with powder exploded. He was only ten feet away and the pieces of rusty iron scythed through the air, some of them catching him full in the face. He fell back with an agonized scream, one eye a sightless, bloody pit.

The second of the mines went off almost at the same time as the first and this proved too much for the youngsters. The one who was uninjured rushed up to his friend, placed an arm round his shoulders and helped him away from the flames. The explosions had spread oil over the third wagon and this too was now burning along with many of the various supplies which had been lying around the place. Looking down at the carnage they had wrought, Archie said, 'Well, I wouldn't o' thought that those carts'll be used to take anybody anywhere.'

'I guess you're right. I'm sorry about that young fellow, though.'

'He shouldn't o' been there in the first place. He got what was comin' to him.'

CHAPTER 7

The dispirited gaggle of girls had been encouraged to get down from the wagons in which they had made the uncomfortable journey south through the territory to the High Peaks. It was beginning to dawn on some of these unfortunate young women that things were not as they had been led to believe when they accepted the offer of new clothes and train tickets down towards New Mexico. They none of them had any cash money to speak of and all had given their signatures to promissory notes for their travel and clothing. Those who had showed any inclination to cut and run had been warned that if they could not pay for the goods and services which had been provided for them, then they would be taken to court and most likely end up in a debtors' gaol until the money expended on them had been fully repaid with interest.

There is a natural human tendency to hope for the best and despite their misgivings, none of the eleven girls who got down from the wagons suspected for a moment the horrible truth about the fate that awaited them. They stood around stretching their limbs and expressing the desire for a little privacy in order to answer calls of nature. Meanwhile, the men who had accompanied them this far conducted some dealings with a new group of rough-looking men. It was when these negotiations were just about at an end that there were two sharp explosions, which reminded the older men of cannon fire. They looked round uneasily and saw a column of smoke rising into the evening air.

One of those who had delivered the girls said, 'Something's afoot. Anything to do with you men?'

'No ...' began one of the men who had been camping nearby, 'except that that smoke is nigh to where we're staying.'

'Shit,' said another man, 'that's right over by the camp.'

There was general consternation among the comancheros, as it gradually became obvious that there had been fire and explosions at their camp. The members of the other band of comancheros stood laughing at the predicament in which the others found themselves. Then they began preparing to head back north.

'You bastards going to lend a hand?' asked one of the men getting ready to investigate the fire.

'Not our business!' came back the cheerful response.

Six of the men vaulted into the saddle and set off at

a gallop to see what was happening, leaving the other ten to shepherd the girls up into the hills on foot. The evening was not turning out in the least how they had expected it to.

At about the same time that the girls were changing hands up by the foothills of the High Peaks a dozen grim-faced men were saddling up outside Greenhaven's livery stable. Their aim was simple and direct. They hoped to run to earth a man by the name of Brent Cutler and when once they had done so, the intention was to hang him from the nearest tree.

It wasn't often these days that it proved necessary to raise a posse in this way. Most people knew of the reputation of Greenhaven's safety committee and took care to avoid committing any crimes in the general vicinity of the town. Even the comancheros tended to act a little cautiously when they were operating nearby. All but two of the twelve men assembled on this particular occasion were veterans of the War Between the States and it would have been a rash man, or a desperate one, who would have stood in their way this night.

Before they rode out, Seaton addressed a few words to them. He said, 'This man is as slippery and dangerous as they come. I had word of his being in this area and sent four good men to give him a warning. They were going to strip him and turn him loose naked. He chose to shoot them. Well, their deaths are on my conscience and I won't rest easy 'til I've avenged them. One thing I'd say is don't listen to a word this devil says. He might claim to be a sheriff, a lawyer, a senator or I don't know what-all else. Don't any of you pay any heed. We catch him and kill him and there's an end to it.'

The only man in the posse who took no notice at all of this fine speech was Jack Carlton. He knew full well that Seaton was lying through his teeth and, what's more, he had a shrewd suspicion as to what lay behind those lies. Whatever chanced this night, he was sure that he now had a weapon to use against the chief of the vigilance men.

Once they were on the road to Fort James, Carlton rode up until he was alongside Seaton, 'How'll we know this Cutler fellow should we come across him?'

'That's no difficulty,' said Seaton. 'Bob Andrews was there when Ezra was shot. He's with us tonight.'

In fact Carlton had already noticed Andrews' presence and was only using this as a conversational gambit to bring the subject round to Brent Cutler. He said, 'Where'd you hear about this Cutler fellow? You get a letter or something?'

Mark Seaton was not a practised liar and Carlton was pleased to remark that his supposed friend looked distinctly uncomfortable about being asked an outright question in this way. He affected not to notice this and waited patiently to hear what lie Seaton would be able to devise to explain his knowledge of the man from Pharaoh.

After an awkward silence, Seaton coughed and said,

'No, there was no letter. Fellow from Fort James gave me the signal.'

'What, he come by here especially to tell you?' asked Carlton innocently. Although he was gaining a good deal of amusement from the situation, hearing old sober-sides being forced to tell a string of lies, there was more to Carlton's purpose than mere malice. He wished to sow doubt in Mark Seaton's mind and make him feel discomforted. Judging by the look on the lay preacher's face, he was succeeding already in this endeavour. All this was laying the grounds for the time in the not too distant future when he put the bite on Mark Seaton.

After having assured themselves of the complete success of their mission, Archie and Cutler slithered back down the scree and then mounted up. Archie said, 'Well, you did good for a man who don't look to get his hands dirty all that often. I'd say we done as much to put a stick in those boys' wheels as any of your paperwork might have done up at Pharaoh.'

'I suppose I ought to be getting on now. I still have to get to Greenhaven. I only hired this horse for seven days and I'm going to be cutting it a bit fine if I don't get to Greenhaven this night.'

The older man thought this over for a bit and then said, 'Tell you what, son, I could do with visiting town myself. Why not come back to stay another night with me and then we'll both ride over there in the morning.

You'd not be getting much in the way of your work done there at this time of night.'

'It's a kind offer, but I feel that I've imposed upon your hospitality too long already.'

Archie snorted in derision. 'Imposed nothing! I been enjoying your visit. Don't see all that many folks, truth to tell. Come on, stay tonight and we'll ride to Greenhaven tomorrow, first thing.'

'Well, if you're sure that I won't be in the way—'

'That's settled then.'

The half dozen riders who reached the site of the attack first were appalled by what they saw. All three of the wagons were charred to cinders and most of their other gear had also been reduced to ashes. It was when attention turned to the two youngsters who had been left to guard the base that feelings really began to run high. When one of the oldest and toughest of the men, the closest thing they had to a leader, saw the ruined face of the boy who had been caught in the blast, he swore violently and at great length. 'This,' he announced in a deadly voice, 'this, as you all know, is my sister's son. She wanted me to make a man of him. Look what those beasts have done to him!' The others gazed upon the empty eye socket from which blood trickled down the boy's face like tears.

'It was the vigilantes,' shouted one of the men. 'Those bastards from Greenhaven did this, without a doubt.'

There was silence at this. The very same idea had struck them all, but this man was the first to speak it out loud. Nobody said anything for a few seconds, then the man whose nephew had been so grievously injured, spoke again, saying, 'I call on all gods and men to hear this oath. I will hunt down those who did this and kill them with my own two hands. Who is with me?'

It is strange, the mental gymnastics that even an honest and God-fearing man can perform with his conscience when the need arises. Mark Seaton was hoping that the man called Cutler would be dead before the dawn, but he was squeamish about getting blood on his own hands. His wish was that they might come upon the lawyer and that he would make a fight of it and be killed in the process. Then Seaton would be able to persuade himself in a short while that he was guiltless of the fellow's death and perhaps be able to forget about the matter.

The twelve riders approached the low hills which marked the approach to the High Peaks, when one of them remarked, 'Anybody else smell smoke?'

They reined in and everybody sniffed, until it was agreed that there was indeed something burning, not far from them. 'Could it be a camp-fire?' asked Seaton. 'If so, we're maybe on the right track.'

'Wouldn't o' thought so,' said Bob Andrews. 'Smells like oil as well. Something's to do up yonder in the hills. You want that we should look into it?'

Before he was able to frame an answer, there came the drumming of hoof beats and, as they watched, a small body of riders came down from the nearby hills and began cantering towards them.

When the rest of the comancheros arrived with the girls, plans had already been laid. A couple of men would be enough to take care of the girls. Allowing that the young man who had lost an eye could be left out of the reckoning fifteen men were left to go after those who had caused such damage to the interests of the band; it was becoming tolerably clear to all of them that there was no way on earth that they could get these girls to walk something over sixty miles on foot to the border. All else apart, all it would take would be for some busybody to spot what they were about and then there might be trouble. Keeping the young women out of sight in wagons was not just to save their shoe-leather; it prevented folk asking what these men were up to with such young girls, where they were taking them and a whole host of other, similar such foolish questions.

'There was nobody down on the plain other than those men we dealt with,' said the uncle of the wounded boy. 'Means that those that did this were up there, on the slopes. The boys say that something rolled down from up in that direction.' He gestured towards the ridge where Brent Cutler had lately been crouching. 'I say that five men ride fast, down to the plain and then round the hills. The rest of us will go on foot, climb up the slopes and see if we can find any sign of those vigilantes.'

Some of the men thought privately that those who had caused this destruction would most likely be long gone by now, but it seemed worth a try. Five of them mounted up and then set off at a brisk canter, leaving the little valley and heading down to the lower ground at the foot of the hills. They struck lucky, or so they first thought, almost at once, finding a group of riders at rest, watching the hills. Without a word, they spurred on their horses and headed for these men, to see what they were about.

There was a horrible inevitability about the course of events, when once the comancheros became aware of the vigilance men sitting there on their horses, seemingly waiting for them. They reined in about forty feet from the other men and one of them called out, 'You sons of whores think that you can behave so and not suffer for it?'

This was so unexpected, that for a moment, Mark Seaton was speechless with surprise. Then he recollected himself and shouted back sternly, 'We'll have no cursing or anything of that sort. What ails you?' Like the other men in the posse, he had no idea what all this tended towards, but he was surely not going to allow these rough-looking characters to insult him with impunity.

The sun had now dipped entirely below the horizon, but it was not yet dark. The two groups of riders faced each other and for a brief moment, things could have gone either way. But one of the comancheros had not the patience or wit to play things slowly and he went for the pistol at his hip. Whether he was intending to start shooting or was perhaps simply making a show of bravado, nobody would ever know. As he drew his gun, Bob Andrews slid his rifle out of the scabbard at the front of his saddle and worked the lever to put a round in the breech. The metallic click acted as a declaration of intent, because the rest of the posse went for their weapons as soon as they heard it. Seeing the men in front of them all pulling iron, the other four comancheros also went for their guns and by then it was obvious to everybody that there was going to be a firefight.

Later that night, not one of the men who took part in the brief and bloody battle could say with any degree of confidence which side began the shooting. Not that it really mattered. When the crash of gunfire began, it was not possible to discern individual shots; the sound was like one continuous roll of thunder; a sustained roar, which stopped as abruptly as it had started. Three of the comancheros were dead and two of the posse had also been hit; one was mortally injured. For all the comancheros' familiarity with firearms, it was the ex-soldiers who proved to be the deadlier shots. The two surviving members of the gang were suddenly and shockingly aware that they were now outnumbered better than five to one. They turned tail and galloped back towards the hills.

The pall of smoke hung about the posse like a fog. Bob Andrews had fallen from his horse and lay on the ground without moving. Another man had taken a ball through his shoulder. These two were the only casualties. A few yards away, a third horse was wandering aimlessly round with its rider slumped forward, groaning piteously. Mark Seaton said, 'Fetch that wounded man nigh to me.'

One of the others went over, took the reins of the horse and led it to Seaton. The man was barely able to remain in the saddle, swaying to and fro as though he might at any moment plummet to the ground. His shirt was dark with blood and from the look of it the ball had probably taken him through a lung. He was breathing rapidly and shallowly and if Mark Seaton was any judge of such things, then here was a man who was not long for this world. 'Well,' he said to the man, 'it's all up with you. Tell me, why did you and your friends fire on us?'

'You screwed us....'

Seaton leaned forward in the saddle, because the man's voice was feeble and reedlike. He had been taken through the lung for sure. 'Screwed you?' asked Seaton, wincing at the obscenity, as though it left a bad taste on his tongue, 'I don't follow you. What do you say we did?'

'Burned ... burned us out'.'

'What? What are you talking of?'

But the man didn't speak again. Instead, he slumped forward even more and one of the posse dismounted swiftly and eased him down to the ground, where he proceeded to die.

'What d'you make of it?' somebody asked Seaton.

'I don't rightly know,' he said slowly, 'but something's amiss. I don't know if there's any more of those scoundrels up there in the hills, but I say we'd best get back to town and rally more people in the morning. There's mischief afoot.' For some reason, he felt profoundly uneasy, as though he had a presentiment of his own death. It was absurd, but he felt the need to get back to his own home as soon as he was able. Brent Cutler could wait; there was something worse in the wind and he didn't have any notion as to what it might be. As if to echo his sombre mood, there was a rumble of distant thunder and a brief, flickering purple light somewhere over the mountains.

'There's a storm coming,' said Jack Carlton.

In the strange home of the old man called Archie, Brent Cutler listened to the wind picking up outside. He said, 'You must be pretty well proof against all kinds of weather in here?'

'You got that right, boy,' said the old man. 'Nary a drop o' rain nor so much as a breath of wind ever get in here. Warm in the winter and cool in the summer, into the bargain.'

'They say folks long ago used to live so, meaning in caves and suchlike.'

'So I heard. We best talk of the morning. You don't want to start telling all the world and his brother your name and business when we reach town, you hear what I'm tellin' you? Put yourself and me both in hazard.'

'I'm not sure of the best way to approach things,' said Cutler slowly, 'but whatever way it falls, I'll take care not to bring you into the business.'

'Huh! I'm old enough to take care of my own self. You're little more than a boy; you'll get ate up alive if you don't take care.'

'I have a job to do. More than that, I have a crow to pluck with that Mark Seaton. I didn't realize until you told me one or two things, that I might already know the man. I can't rest easy 'til I've looked into this and figured out all the angles. But it's my affair and I'll not drag anybody else into it.'

CHAPTER 8

The comancheros now found themselves in a grim and unenviable position. When the riders returned, it was to find their comrades hastening back from their search on foot and wondering what all the shooting might portend.

The deaths of two of their number was sad, but it confirmed absolutely, at least in their own minds, that the earlier attack on their camp had indeed been the work of the vigilantes. Juarez, whose nephew had been injured in the earlier attack on their camp, said, 'It is, without the shadow of a doubt, the work of those bastards from Greenhaven.' There was little point in haring off after the men now, not without first setting down together and figuring out a plan of campaign. In the meantime, they surveyed the wreckage of their possessions.

The three wagons in which they had proposed to move the girls south to the border had been reduced

to piles of charred ashes. A similar fate had befallen
the harnesses, rifles and other gear, which had been
stowed nearby. They had also suffered casualties and
in addition to these misfortunes, were almost out of
money due to the large sum which had changed hands
a few hours ago in order for them to acquire the eleven
girls.

The men took counsel among themselves, hoping
to mitigate in some way the disaster which had befallen
them. The girls whom they now had charge of were
even younger than they had been led to believe. In
fact two were just fourteen years of age; three of them
were fifteen and none of the others above eighteen.
Anybody who caught a glimpse of these fresh young
white girls in the company of swarthy bandits such
as them would fully apprehend the situation at once.
Anybody who guessed that white slavers were in their
area would be certain-sure to raise the alarm. Getting
their cargo to the Rio Grande on foot was hardly to be
thought of, even if they travelled by night. Long before
the sixty-mile journey was completed, they would find
themselves fighting for their lives against soldiers or
vigilantes and such an encounter would most likely end
with every mother's son of them hanging from trees.

It was Juarez who came up with the scheme which
might, as the saying went, enable them to pull the meat
from the fire without burning their fingers. He said,
'We owe the men of Greenhaven a bad turn for their
work this night. We need wagons too, to carry these,'

he gestured at the girls, 'to Mexico, without their being seen. The answer is clear enough.'

'Tell us then, brother!' said one of the men, who was not overly pleased to see Juarez setting himself up as their captain.

'Why, the matter is simplicity itself. To speak plainly, we descend upon that town tomorrow night and set it to the torch. Then, while those who live there are racing back and forth like headless chickens, trying to save their families and houses, we take the wagons that we need.'

There was dead silence after Juarez had spoken, as sixteen violent and ruthless men worked the idea over in their minds, looking for any way that it might bring about their own deaths. They saw none. True, one or two of them might fall if there was gunplay, but that was no more than the fortunes of war. They had, once before, had occasion to burn a village and that had gone well enough. The towns hereabouts were built almost entirely of wood and blazed merrily once a fire was kindled against their walls.

Since there were no dissenting voices, it was accepted that this would be the course of action. There seemed little else that could be done other than cutting their losses and abandoning the girls, hoping perhaps to take down a mail coach on the road to gain a little capital. Set against this was that by doing as Juarez suggested, they would be showing that they were men who were not to be injured and killed with impunity. The character of helpless victim was one which sat ill with these men. At the very least, they would have to revenge themselves upon those who had harmed their interests so wantonly.

The following day dawned sullen and dark, with the leaden skies holding a promise of rain to come. Archie was up and about early, as was his wont. He chaffed Cutler when the young man showed no signs of stirring before seven, saying, 'You ain't working in some fancy office now, boy. There'll be no fine carriage to take you to work, neither. You want to get to town with me, then you best bestir yourself and wash. I dare say you'll be wanting coffee and vittles too, afore we set out.'

'We're leaving at once?' asked Brent Cutler groggily. 'What's the hurry?'

'Hurry is that the day's half worn away and I got a heap of things need doing,' replied the old man tartly. 'Now just move yourself.'

After they had made a good breakfast, Archie lit his pipe and said in a conversational tone of voice, 'You riding the vengeance trail?'

The direct question was unexpected and for a second or two, Cutler hardly knew how to answer. He said finally, 'What makes you to think so?'

'Ah,' said Archie, a satisfied smile on his face, 'I thought so. Man answers your question with one of his own, you can take oath as he's something to hide.'

Cutler thought this over for a few seconds before

saying slowly, 'I don't know what put it into your mind to ask about this, but no. I don't think I'm seeking vengeance. Looking for answers to one or two questions, maybe.'

'Just as I thought. There's more to this than a business transaction.'

Although he had not fully untangled the threads, even in his own mind, it seemed to Cutler that it might not be a bad idea to share with this strange man what he now knew. Haltingly, because the pain of what had happened those twelve years ago was still as fresh and raw as ever, he told Archie about the lynching of his father. When he had finished his narrative, during the whole course of which the other man had not once interrupted him, Cutler said, 'When I read the documents on this trip and saw the name Seaton, it half brought something to mind, though I couldn't have said what. Then when you told me about this marshal who was killed, everything fitted neatly together.'

'Yes, it weren't hard to calculate that something was going through your mind when you asked if I could recollect the name of the town where that occurred.'

The two of them sat there in companionable silence, the old man sucking on his pipe. At length, Cutler asked, 'What can you tell me about Seaton? Do you think he would have lynched a man he knew to be innocent?'

'Not when I knew him well, no. But men change over the years. I couldn't answer for his character these days. He was always a stiff-necked beggar, worrying about his neighbour's sins more than his own.'

There didn't appear to be much else to say and so they saddled up their horses and set off west towards Greenhaven.

It was disturbing to Mark Seaton that the representative from the District Attorney's office had still not shown up yet. He was hoping that some misfortune had befallen the fellow on the road, but still inwardly fretting that at any moment a stranger would fetch up and announce to all the town who he was and what he had come for. It would have eased Seaton's mind to have taken this Cutler on the road and disposed of him out of sight of the town. He was not sure that once people had spoken to and broken bread with the man, that they would countenance his summary execution. It was a real conundrum.

As a rule, folk in Greenhaven were bright and cheerful early on a May morning, but today it was as though a cloud hung over the town. The deaths of four citizens in less than forty-eight hours had had a bad effect upon the place. The weather didn't help matters, either. Rain had been expected the previous night, but it hadn't arrived. Judging from the roiling black thunderclouds up towards the High Peaks, though, it wouldn't be long before there was a regular downpour.

As he trotted his horse along Main Street, Seaton scarcely noticed a white-haired old man, accompanied by a younger man who was smartly and soberly dressed. He had more important things on his mind that scrutinizing every passing stranger. Had he looked closer, he might have realized that he had at one time known the old man pretty well.

'Yonder's Seaton,' said Archie, 'him coming along now on that grey mare.'

Cutler observed closely the man thus indicated and felt an electric shock of recognition run through him when he looked at the man's face. He was instantly transported back to that terrible night in his childhood when he had witnessed the death of his father. 'I recognize him,' he said in a soft undertone to the man walking at his side. 'Mother of God, I recall him now as though it had been yesterday. It was he that organized my father's death.'

'Keep your voice down,' said Archie. 'There's no point in tipping your hand, leastways not 'til you know what you aim to do.'

'As to that, I hardly know myself.'

'Want some advice?'

'I'd be right glad of it.'

'Then here it is. Don't go racing after Seaton right now and making a ruckus. Let folk here in town see you and get your measure. That way, if there's any talk o' just tucking you quietly out of the way, maybe people won't wear it, if you follow me. You won't be some stranger who can be bundled off in the wilderness and silenced.'

*

Although it wouldn't do to let others see it, Juarez felt terrible about the blinding and disfigurement of his nephew. He had always taken an interest in the boy and acted as his protector. Now, while the youngster was in his own care, he had lost one eye and had his handsome face torn open in half a dozen places as well. Now that day had broken, it was possible to assess the full extent of the boy's injuries and they did not look at all good. In truth, he needed the services of a doctor, but that was unthinkable at the moment. They would just have to hope and pray that none of the wounds became poisonous. A wave of fury swept through the bandit as he thought about the actions of those vigilantes. The two men who had been shot dead last night were one thing. This had been a fair fight and they had fallen in battle. The raid on the camp, though, that was something else again; a cowardly and unmanly piece of work.

The boy was sleeping fitfully and Juarez found himself unable to take his eyes off that terrible, empty eye socket. Well, he would see that this injury was amply recompensed in blood and fire. It might not restore sight to his sister's son's eye, but it would make Juarez himself feel a whole lot better.

Juarez strolled over to three of the men who were sitting smoking and glaring around them moodily. He said, 'We need a man to stay here and set a watch on the women.' None of the three looked at all enthusiastic about undertaking such a task and one of them hawked and spat.

This man looked up at Juarez and said, 'You're taking a lot upon yourself, my friend. "You" need a man? Are you our captain?'

'By no means. But we all want to get the wherewithal to take those girls over into Chihauhau, is it not so?'

'It might be so. But I'll be damned if I stay here when we ride tonight.'

Every one of the men whose views he canvassed expressed the same opinion as that first. Not one of them, even the young fellow of seventeen, would consent to remain in the camp while the others set off to burn down the town. In the end, there was nothing for it but to dragoon his nephew into undertaking the guard duty. In a way, it made sense, because the lad would certainly be no manner of use to them; he'd be more of a hindrance than a help.

The girls were getting fidgety and restless, wanting to know when they'd be getting to town. Some of them, chiefly the younger ones, still believed that they would be acting on a stage or, at the very least, dancing in some kind of cabaret show or musical theatre. They were impatient to reap all the supposed benefits of their new careers: the fine clothes, money to spend, admiring beaux and all the rest of it. Tempers were fraying and their latest guardians had little time for this nonsense, telling the young women that there were worse things than being stuck up in the hills with no

shelter. This sounded so ominous, that even the bright-
est and liveliest of the girls felt disinclined to ask just
what was meant by this. By the end of the day, all but
one or two had correctly divined that they would have
been better off had they stayed in their dull homes
and resisted the lure of the fine lifestyle being dangled
before them by the men who had recruited them from
the farms of Montana and Nebraska.

The plan that Juarez formulated with his comrades
during the day was a simple one which, properly executed, might prove devastatingly effective. After dark,
the fifteen men would ride down to Greenhaven. They
would not approach the town as one body of horsemen
– such a proceeding being likely to arouse the liveliest
suspicions among those who saw them. Comancheros
were not the most popular of men in those parts and
the sight of fifteen riding into a town would almost certainly draw forth the vigilantes to see what they were
about.

Once they were on the outskirts of the town,
the men would scout round and locate some handy
wagons, such as might be driven off in a hurry. The
most likely spot for acquiring such vehicles would be
the livery stable. While some were doing this, others
would be preparing to raise a dozen fires simultane-
ously at many different places, including commercial
premises and domestic dwelling houses. In the ensuing
panic, with everybody fighting furiously to prevent the
whole, entire town from being burned to the ground,

it should be easy enough to harness up the wagons and take them, using stolen horses to draw them.

The great drawback in this scheme was of course falling foul of the vigilance men. However, they too would be too busy saving the town to think of forming up a posse or anything of that sort. Or so at least Juarez and the others hoped.

It was drawing near to the time, thought Brent Cutler regretfully, that he and Archie would be parting. He didn't know what business the other had in town, but it would presumably be better conducted without his being present. After they had seen Mark Seaton ride by, Cutler said, 'I suppose here is where we part company?'

'How so?'

'I thought you'd private business here?'

Archie looked at him sideways and said, 'You're a green young thing. It wouldn't sit easy with me to abandon you here. You want that we stay together for the day, I'm agreeable.'

Relief flooded through the young lawyer and he began to express this in words, only to be cut short in the most irritable way by the older man. 'Yes, yes. There's no need to get all flowery. You got money for a hotel room?'

'I have money to disburse for accommodation. Is there a hotel in this town?'

'Money to disburse for accommodation! Lord, you

sound like a dictionary. They let rooms over the *Lucky Man*. Used to have a whorehouse above the saloon, but Seaton put paid to that. Come on, I'll show you the way.'

The barkeep at the *Lucky Man* was only too pleased to rent two rooms for the night. It was a rare enough occurrence. Cutler tried to pay for Archie's room, as well as his own, but this offer was brusquely refused: 'I ain't yet in need o' charity from any man!'

Archie went off to see whoever he had come to town to deal with, reminding Cutler that it would be no bad thing for him to make himself agreeable to those he met. The young man wandered round Greenhaven, trying to get a feel for the town. It seemed a steady and reliable kind of place and for all that he was there to overturn their current arrangements for the maintenance of good order, he was forced to concede that whatever they were doing appeared to be working well enough. In the course of his perambulations, he took good care to be as pleasant and good natured as he could be, ensuring that those whom he encountered were favourably impressed with him and not likely subsequently to think him a dangerous villain fit only to be hanged.

The next day, having established himself a little, he would call on Seaton and lay his cards on the table. It was a pity that there was no telegraph office in the town, or he could perhaps have sought advice from his boss. The fact that Archie was apparently determined to stay with him and support him was a source of great comfort, though; almost like having an older relative near to hand.

Despite the four deaths, life in Greenhaven went on that day much as usual. Any death is regrettable, but life continues and already other concerns were pressing the average citizen of the town; such things as earning a living, providing for one's children, dealing with creditors, putting food on the table, keeping a roof overhead and the hundred and one other normal, everyday worries. By nightfall, the battle with the comancheros and murder of two men by a dangerous confidence trickster were no longer in the forefront of most people's minds.

Although he wasn't himself a total abstainer from intoxicating liquor, Cutler seldom drank and had only once or twice seen the inside of a saloon, preferring books to whiskey and beer. That evening, though, Archie talked him into visiting the bar at the *Lucky Man*. 'The more men as see you and judge for themselves how likely you are to be a killer, the better it will be when you beard Seaton in his lair,' was the way in which he expressed this. So, with considerable reluctance, Brent Cutler found himself that evening supping a glass of porter in the crowded barroom.

A number of people recognized Archie and greeted him by name. He in turn introduced them to Cutler as a friend of his and by the end of the evening everybody was getting on famously, which had of course

been Archie's intention all along. As the evening pro-
gressed, it became increasingly clear just how cunning
Archie had been. By ten o'clock, they were all such
good friends, that nobody would have consented for a
moment to seeing old Archie's friend dragged out the
saloon and hanged. It also became obvious just what
lengths Archie had gone to to protect Cutler from
danger, perhaps even hazarding his own standing in
the town as he did so.

'Let's drink up, gentleman,' said the barkeep, as the
hour of ten approached. 'Come on now, I don't want
any friction with the safety committee.'

'Come on, Jim,' cried one of the drinkers, 'just
another quarter-hour won't do no harm.'

'Not to you maybe, but I already had Mark Seaton
in here, reading me the Riot Act. No siree, I aim to
have this place closed up promptly at ten.'

While this good-natured banter was taking place
in the *Lucky Man*, four strangers were walking around
the streets outside. They had divided up into pairs
and were taking pains not to attract attention to
themselves. These men were the advance party of the
comancheros and their single aim was to locate two or
three suitable carts or wagons which they might steal.

The other eleven men were prowling around the
outskirts of the town, marking down buildings which
looked as though they would be likely to burn without
too much trouble. They too were divided up into
parties of no more than two or three. One of these

little groups, that consisting of Juarez and two other men, had a rare stroke of good fortune while investigating an alley off Main Street. They discovered a shed at back of Jack Carlton's general store, which, when the lock was forced, proved to contain drums of lamp oil.

'I say that the Mother of God has smiled upon our enterprise,' said Juarez facetiously. 'There must be forty or fifty gallons here.' He delved into the darkness and emerged clutching some earthenware pitchers. 'We can decant the oil into these jugs. I might say as there's enough lamp oil here to make a fine blaze. With good fortune and providing the rain holds off for a few hours, we should be able to destroy their damned town entirely.'

CHAPTER 9

The crime of fire-raising, which lawyers call arson, has traditionally been seen as deserving of the most condign punishment; up to and including the death penalty. The reason isn't hard to fathom. Fire is indiscriminate and when once you set fire to one field or house, it can swiftly spread and destroy a good deal of property and claim the lives of innocent people. The course of action which Juarez and his companions were about to embark upon would be enough to get them hanged practically anywhere in the Union. In a town like Greenhaven, with such a strict set of vigilance men, they were all but sitting up and begging to be lynched if they were detected in the act.

As the patrons of the *Lucky Man* wandered off into the night, they were wholly unaware that three men were at that very moment lurking behind the saloon. They had piled up pieces of wood, scraps of paper and handfuls of straw against the wooden wall and had splashed lamp oil liberally over this collection of garbage. Having done this, the men moved on to the back of the general store and repeated the process there. Meanwhile, across the town, other little bonfires were being prepared near barns, houses and other wooden buildings. When the moment came to strike, twenty fires would spring up at once, in widely separated parts of Greenhaven. With no official firefighters in the town and little provision for such an emergency, the results would be catastrophic.

And still the storm, which had now been brewing in the mountains for over twenty-four hours, had not reached Greenhaven. The rumble of thunder was now more or less continuous and growing louder by the hour, but as yet, not a drop of rain had fallen. There had been no rain in the area since the spring had begun and all the buildings were as dry as tinder. Even without the mischief being planned by the comancheros, there was a perpetual risk of fires starting from something as inconsequential as a discarded cigar. If the gallons of oil were to take, then it was by no means improbable that the whole town could go up in smoke.

Archie had taken a room in the same corridor as Cutler's and before they turned in for the night, he begged the favour of a few words with him. When he entered Cutler's room, his eyebrows rose as he surveyed the rich, but faded curtains and the fly-spotted pier glass at one end of the room. He said, 'I reckon you can tell that this place used to be a cathouse. I should think your room must have belonged to a twenty-dollar whore.'

'Looks that way,' said Cutler, with a laugh. 'Thanks for introducing me to all those people tonight. I know what you were doing and I'm grateful for it.'

Caught out in a charitable endeavour, the old man looked abashed and said, 'Hell, that's nothing. Anyways, that ain't what I wanted to talk 'bout. You brought that pistol with you that you had when I met you? Leastways, I surely hope you have.'

Cutler bent down and fumbled in the carpet bag in which he carried his change of clothes. 'Yes, here it is.'

'Show it me.'

Archie took the gun and broke open the cylinder; checking to see that all the cartridges were unfired. Then he spun the cylinder and checked the action of the trigger a couple of times. 'You know how to shoot?' he asked.

'I shot two men just before I met you. I can shoot well enough.'

'You got a rig for that thing? Or were you fixing to stick it in your belt like some *desperado*?'

'I don't have a gunbelt, no.'

Archie stumped out of the room and went across the corridor to his own room. He returned with a holster and thick leather belt. In the other hand, he had a cardboard box of forty-five shells. As he crossed the threshold to the room, he paused and cocked his head to one side. 'What's wrong?' said Cutler.

'Listen, son, you ain't out o' the woods yet, not by a long sight. That was the sound of shooting, away 'cross town, by the sound of it. You best get this on now, just on the off chance that somebody takes agin you. Understand?'

It was as Cutler was buckling on the belt and filling his pockets with spare cartridges that they heard a shout from nearby. Somebody was yelling, 'Fire! Fire!'

The storm that had been threatening for so long looked as though it was going to arrive at any moment. Lightning was flickering through the clouds to the east and it surely wouldn't be long before the rain began. The plan had been to fire the town at midnight, but waiting an hour struck Juarez as tempting fate. The wind was picking up and the cracks of thunder and flashes of lightning were separated by only a few seconds. The wind would help fan the flames, but the rain would be the ruination of the plan. At a little after eleven, according to the clock on the church tower, Juarez said, 'It would be madness to wait further. All of you, go and set your fires.' The two that he spoke to went off to pass the word to the others.

The streets were almost deserted. It was a weekday evening, which meant that most folks went early to bed any way and on top of that, the wind was blowing hard and rain was expected at any moment. It was no time to be out and about; not unless you had good reason to be so. The fifteen comancheros moved through the dark streets like ghosts, unmarked by any of the residents of Greenhaven.

Two of the men had another job. They had been scouting round in search of some carriages or wagons which could be used to transport the eleven girls south to the border. At first, things had not looked too promising. It was when they peered into a large barn on the edge of town that they hit pay dirt, for within were two wagons which looked to be in perfect condition. They were just standing there, side by side; two old fashioned 'prairie schooners'. It was the most tremendous stroke of luck and the two of them could at first scarcely believe the evidence of their senses.

Really, the wagons were meant to be pulled by four oxen or horses, but at a pinch it wasn't difficult to make do with two apiece. This would mean that when they left town, each of the wagons would have to carry the two men whose horses had been pressed into service. It would be a finely balanced operation to ensure that the men of the town were so preoccupied with fighting the threats to their town that they had no time to spare to challenge those riding away with these wagons. They would have to harness the wagons up and be ready to ride off at the height of the fires.

There was every hope that the comancheros' plan would be successful and when it failed, it was not through any fault of those who devised it. As the others were starting fires in many different spots, the men whose job was to commandeer the wagons led the four horses to the barn and then opened the doors. They were taken aback to find the owner of the property which they were about to carry off, standing behind the doors, in the darkness, as though he were waiting for them. In his arms, he cradled a sawn-off scattergun.

'Saw you fellows, poking about earlier. Didn't think nobody had seen you, huh? Well lemme tell you, nobody steals from Jed Arkwright, no sir. Not never!'

It is generally a mistake to get carried away with one's own eloquence, especially when facing two desperate bandits who would kill a man as soon as bandy words with him. Without troubling to say a word in defence of their actions, both comancheros pulled their pistols and began firing. The man who called himself Jed Arkwright fell back, dying. In his final extremity, though, his finger twitched convulsively, loosing off both barrels of his shotgun. The pellets from this went wide of their target, but the brief exchange of fire was audible across the whole of Greenhaven.

The sharp crack of pistols, followed almost instantly by the dull boom of the scattergun caused dogs to bark and windows to be thrown up, as people leaped from their beds to see what was happening on the streets of their quiet town. It had been some years since anybody had dared disturb the peace in this way.

One of those who was peering out into the darkness saw a flickering orange light behind the saloon. He rubbed his eyes and established that this was more than somebody carrying a lantern. By this time, the flames were leaping high enough to be clearly visible. He yelled at the top of his voice, 'Fire! Fire!'

At the sound of gunfire, Juarez began swearing furiously. He knew immediately that his carefully laid plans were about to unravel. Nevertheless, for want of any alternative, he carried on splashing oil over a pile of junk behind somebody's house before setting it alight. It might yet be all right, he thought. That was before he felt the first drop of rain falling from the clouds which hung low over the town.

'Hurry it up and stop fooling round with that belt,' said Archie urgently. 'There's mischief afoot. Turn down that lamp and don't go nigh to the window 'til you done so.'

Swiftly, Cutler trimmed the lamp and went to the window. He saw at once that flames were licking the wall twenty feet below. 'There's a fire for sure,' he said. 'We best rouse the place.'

'I wish I'd o' brought my rifle with me,' declared the old man fretfully.

'Your rifle? What use would that be in fighting a fire?'

'It ain't just the fire as I'm afeared of. There's more to this than meets the eye.'

Together, the two men ran through the corridors, banging on every door and yelling that there was a fire. The building, though, was all but deserted, with only the barkeep and his wife sleeping on the premises.

When he was awoken, that individual raced downstairs. The *Lucky Man* was his livelihood, life savings and security for his old age all rolled up into one. He didn't aim to have it destroyed by fire, not without taking any steps necessary to avert catastrophe.

The four of them, the woman doing as much as any of the men, managed to bring the fire outside under control by filling buckets, ewers and even vases with water and dowsing the flames with them. As they worked, the rain began, which aided matters. By the time the fire was extinguished, all four of them had come to a similar conclusion: this had been a deliberate act. In effect, a bonfire had been constructed against the rear wall of the saloon, the obvious intention being to burn down the building. 'It don't make a speck of sense,' said the barkeep. 'Who'd want to burn down this place?'

After killing the owner of the two wagons, the men wasted no time in harnessing up the horses to them. They knew that after gunplay things often tended to get a little ugly and lawbreakers tended to have a hard time of it in that town. Once the wagons were ready, they jumped up and set them moving. It had been agreed that they would pick up the owners of the other horses down at the eastern end of Main Street. It would be slow travelling in these things and they would have to hope that the fires that had been set would keep the vigilantes busy to give them a head start in escaping from the town. One thing was certain; they would need to travel all night now. There would, by morning, be a large number of very angry men in Greenhaven.

The sound of shooting had alerted many men to the fact that something uncommon was taking place in their town. The members of the safety committee had a standing arrangement for such an event and when an unforeseen emergency like this erupted, it was the agreed thing that they would muster outside the general store, which occupied a central position on Main Street. After they had hastily dressed, some dozen of these men began making their way through the town to Main Street. As they went, they could see here and there the glow of flames. It was plainly obvious that something very serious was happening and so they did not go off to investigate, but carried on to their meeting place. As they went they shouted out to rouse their neighbours, calling, 'Fire! Get from your beds, the town's in danger!'

As they reached the general store, the scale of the threat was still not clear to the men; most of them thought that this might just be a sort of hooliganism or high jinks by some young folk. It was when two covered wagons came careening around the corner and began rumbling full pelt down Main Street towards them, that they knew that this was going to be a night to remember.

Mark Seaton was among the first to reach the store and welcomed the others as they arrived. As usual, he was faultlessly dressed in black garb, which hinted at a clerical background. Nobody had ever seen Seaton dishevelled or even wearing anything more casual than his regular, black, Sunday-go-to-meeting suits. When Seaton saw the two wagons thundering down the street in their direction, he didn't hesitate for a moment. You could say a lot of hard things about Mark Seaton, that he was a stiff-necked, self-righteous and humourless individual, among other things, but nobody had ever questioned his courage. He stepped straight out into the middle of the street and held up his hand, shouting at the same time, 'Whoa, there!'

The twelve men standing outside the general store watched in awestruck horror, it being tolerably clear to them that those driving the wagons so furiously down Main Street had not the slightest intention of halting their vehicles. Nobody felt able to interfere with Seaton, though, and if he chose to get himself killed in this way, well that was his affair. For a moment, they were all frozen in a tableau, watching the tragedy unfold before them.

Just as it seemed quite certain that the town would shortly be seeking a new leader for their safety committee, there was a blur of movement. A shadowy figure shot past the men standing by the store and cannoned into Seaton, knocking him to one side. The wheels of one of the wagons passed only inches from Seaton's legs as he lay sprawled in the dust. Then they had passed and Seaton, who had resigned himself to death, turned to look at the man who lay next to him.

The reason that Seaton had appeared on the streets looking as starched and proper as ever was that he had not been to bed that night. Instead, he had paced his house in an agony at the wicked course into which he had fallen. It was not only that he was set fair to lose his position as leading citizen of Greenhaven; he had actually sought an innocent man's death for his own purposes. More than that, he had been directly responsible for the deaths of the two members of the safety committee, who he had set after Brent Cutler. After praying about this weighty business, he had resolved to step down from his position of authority the following day and make a public speech of repentance in the chapel on the following Sabbath.

Having, with a heavy heart, come to these decisions, Seaton made his way, when once the alarm was raised, to Main Street. It was when he saw the two wagons bearing down that he made a split second choice and leapt in front of them. For a moment, he had forgotten all the scriptural teaching, that touching upon suicide, and saw a quick and clean way out of the disgrace which was about to engulf him.

When he realized that he was not, after all, about to die that very minute, Seaton got to his feet and dusted down his clothing. The young man who had knocked him down and delivered him from the awful sin of self-destruction did the same and the two men stood facing each other in the middle of the street. The rain was falling in earnest now, which perhaps meant that there was no urgency in arranging to fight the fires which had been seen. Seaton said, 'Well, I guess I owe you a debt of gratitude. You saved my life.'

'It's nothing to speak of. I thought you were in peril and I acted. There's no more to it than that.'

The man who had rescued him was staring at Seaton with what struck him as an intense, almost hungry look that made him feel uncomfortable. He said, 'New to the town, are you? I don't recollect your face.'

'My name is Brent Cutler. You hanged my father some twelve years back.'

Stunned, Mark Seaton stood gazing stupidly at the man who he had come to think of as his own personal and particular Nemesis. Hearing mention of hanging in connection with the name Cutler brought it all flooding back to him now. He knew that the name Cutler had rung a bell somewhere. He even recollected the name of the town they had carried out that hanging in. Grant's Landing. But what strange freak of chance had brought the man's son to his own town now, to relieve him of his post? Seaton looked into Cutler's eyes and said in a resigned voice, 'You'll have come for revenge, maybe?'

Before Cutler was able to reply, one of the men by the store shouted to them, 'We going after those wagons or what?'

'Are you with us, Mr Cutler?' asked Seaton. 'Leastways for now?'

'Yes, I am. I work for the District Attorney and

maintaining the law is my job.'

'Then let's see what's going on.'

The body of vigilantes moved off at a brisk pace in the direction that the wagons had taken.

The rain, which was now pouring down in a veritable torrent, had proved the ruination of Juarez's scheme. The fires were going out and the town was boiling over like a disturbed ant hill. If the comancheros didn't make tracks, and that right soon, they were likely to meet the wrath of several hundred angry men. When he heard the wagons coming towards where he and the others were waiting, Juarez said, 'You men who're riding the carts, jump up. The rest of you, take horse and we'll be away.'

'There's a bunch of men heading behind them,' observed the man at Juarez' side. 'There'll be killing yet, before we're clear of here.'

'So be it.'

As the wagons approached, those driving them reined in and applied the brakes, which, with a screeching of iron on iron, brought them slowly to a halt. The pursuing men were fifty yards behind and some of them gave shouts of triumph when they saw that the gap separating them from their quarry was fast shrinking. Their pleasure was short-lived though, because a second later they were scattering for cover as a fusillade of fire was sent down the road at them.

Brent Cutler, who was new to this game, was slow off the mark in understanding what the smart move would be, so Seaton grabbed hold of his arm and dragged him over to the boardwalk. Seaton said, 'Lawing in an office is one thing. When shooting starts, it's something else again.'

'Isn't that the truth!' muttered Cutler.

Some of the vigilance men had brought rifles along with them; all had pistols. They began to pour a hail of lead at those who had just opened up on them. The problem was that it was now pitch-dark and a thunderstorm was raging into the bargain. The sound of the shooting was almost drowned by the thunder, which, from the sound of it, gave reason to suppose the storm was now directly overhead. It promised to be a lively and entertaining night – for those fortunate enough to survive it.

CHAPTER 10

The vigilance men were crouched in the shelter of the store fronts and standing in the spaces between the buildings. They had no intention of making a frontal assault on whoever had been shooting at them, but then again, those people in turn were pretty well pinned down by fire and would not be in any hurry to offer their backs as targets to the men who were so intent on catching up with them. The firing had died down a little and was sporadic now, but this was only because both parties were just waiting for a chance to get a clear shot at their opponents.

Brent Cutler had been mulling things over in his mind and a terrible fear was beginning to grip him that he had played some part in precipitating this bloody crisis. Could it really be purely a coincidence that he and Archie had destroyed some wagons a matter of hours ago and that now somebody was making off out of town with a couple of other wagons?

It was while he was musing in this way that he felt a grip on his arm from behind and turned to find Archie standing there. 'That was a damn' fool piece of work,' said the old man, 'jumpin' in front a wagon like that!'

Archie saw who Cutler's companion was and nodded to him. 'Evenin', Seaton.'

'Oh, good evening, Mr Carmichael. I hope you're well?' A stray bullet whined down the street, passing only a yard or two from them.

Archie said, 'Let's save the polite society talk for some other time, hey? I suppose this young fellow's told you what's afoot?'

'I don't mind that he has.'

'Me and him cleaned out a nest of comancheros, just lately. Burned their wagons. Happen they've come here for replacements.'

Seaton's eyes became sharp and he said, 'Comancheros? Where was this? Come on, out with it man.'

'Don't try and buffalo me, Mark Seaton,' said Archie. 'You know well enough it won't answer. T'was up in the foot hills, nigh to the High Peaks.'

While they were talking, the shooting was slackening off even more and some of the nearby men were talking of making a rush and seeing if they could overwhelm those who had been firing at them. Seaton broke off from his conversation with Archie to say, 'Nobody move forward, not without my saying so. Slow and steady does it. Anybody injured?' It appeared that one man had a flesh wound in his arm, but that was the full tally.

'What do you think they were about with their carts, Carmichael?' asked the head of the vigilance men. 'Transporting goods south?'

'Most probable.'

'You can show us where they were based?'

'Course I can. I ain't an idiot yet!'

Seaton said to the men around him, 'Cease fire! Let them go.'

'You say what?' cried one of the men. 'After what they done? You goin' soft or what?'

'Carry on talking so to me and you'll see who's gone soft, Bill Cartwright,' said Seaton in a low, deadly voice. 'Let me catch the man who dares to think or say that I'm going soft.'

There was an awkward silence, broken only by the man who had been foolish enough to use the word 'soft', mumbling that he didn't mean nothing and hoped he'd caused no offence to nobody.

'I'll tell you why we're going to let them go,' explained Seaton patiently. 'Those men are going to be restricted to the pace of those prairie schooners. We can give them half an hour and still overtake them on our horses in a few hours. If there's to be a battle, it'll be on our terms, not theirs. Why don't you men wait 'til those boys have stopped shooting entirely and then go and fetch your horses? And all of you, get rifles too. I aim to get those men without hazarding a hair on any of your heads.'

After telling them to be back there as soon as they might, Seaton said to Archie, 'If I know you, you'll be coming with us?'

'Try and stop me!'

Turning to Cutler, Mark Seaton said, 'You and I have a heap of business to attend to, Mr Cutler, both official and personal. That will keep. Will you ride with me this night or would you rather wait here for us?'

'I'll come with you, sir.'

'Good man. You both have horses?'

It was almost three quarters of an hour later, before everybody was assembled and ready to go. The seventeen riders left town at a steady trot. Some of their wives had turned out to watch them leave and there was fear in their eyes. There had been no shooting in Greenhaven itself for years and nothing even remotely like the gun battle seen that night since the War Between the States. Some of the women looked reproachfully towards Mark Seaton, as though to say, 'We thought you promised to keep this kind of thing from our town!' This at any rate was how Seaton himself interpreted their looks.

The rain showed no sign of letting up and the men were all wearing slickers and broad-brimmed hats. Archie and Cutler had no protection of this sort and it looked as though they were in for a cold, wet night.

One of the band of vigilantes was sweating, despite

the cold and rain. This was Jack Carlton, who guessed that the men who had raided the town that night were the very same men with whom he had lately been trading. If that came to light, the Lord only knew what would become of him. He determined that he would just have to do his level best to ensure that either none of the comancheros caught sight of his face or, if they did, that they didn't live too long afterwards.

'You scared?' asked Archie, as they left the town behind.

'No,' said Cutler thoughtfully, 'I wouldn't say I'm precisely scared. Nervous, maybe.'

'That's good. Means you're more apt to stay alive. Nervous men keep their eyes open for danger and are ready to run if need be. It's the men who aren't scared or nervous that you have to watch. Man in that condition'll do all manner of crazy things. I never saw anything in my life to beat you pushing Seaton clear o' that wagon. Brave? I should say so.'

'Thanks. What are we going to do, would you say?'

'I reckon as that's up to Seaton. He's in charge. I'd be surprised, though, if any of those boys as was fire-raising last night are still breathing come the dawn.'

'You think we'll beat them in a fight?'

'There's some tough men here. Tough'uns among them comancheros too, of course. Not as cold and steady as the men from town, mind. Probably not as good shots, neither.'

It wasn't long before the shadowy forms of the wagons and their accompanying riders could be vaguely discerned through the driving rain. Every so often, there was a break in the clouds and the moon shone down upon the plain, which lay between the town of Greenhaven and the foot hills of the High Peaks. The lumbering wagons slowed the comancheros down until the vigilance men were able to outflank them and ride along at either side; about a quarter mile off from the men they were following. From time to time, one of the comancheros would loose off a shot in their direction, to discourage closer pursuit, but at that range and in those conditions, there was little enough danger of them hitting anybody.

By the time the rain was easing off and it was closer to dawn than to dusk, the hills towards which they were heading came into clearer view. Behind them were the towering range known as the High Peaks. Mark Seaton dropped back and then rode alongside Archie. He said, 'Is this where you attacked their camp?'

'Not far from here. You can see the track leading up between those two hills.'

'Why do you think they were so keen to get hold of carts? Did you see a lot of gear that they might have been moving from one place to the other? I mean things like crates of rifles. That sort of thing.'

Archie thought about this for a space and then said, 'Now that you mention it, no. I didn't see more than bits and pieces. Not enough for them to need three wagons, no. Why d'you ask?'

'I know those rascals. I've hanged a few of them before now. They need those wagons, or they wouldn't have taken such a mad risk coming to town to steal them. I know what they're about.'

'Goin' to share it with us?' asked Archie, a note of irritation in his voice.

'You know as well as I do, Carmichael. They're white slavers. We're much to blame for this, me and the other vigilance men. Not just here but also over in Fort James. All over. Turning a blind eye to wickedness, as long as it's not on our very doorstep. I'll warrant they've got some girls near at hand and they're taking them to Mexico.'

'Are you going to stop them, Mr Seaton?' asked Cutler.

'I'm going to hang them,' said Seaton grimly, 'but we'll need to take them before they get into those hills. I don't fancy fighting on that territory. They know it better than me.'

'We'd best bring 'em to heel, then,' remarked Archie. 'Another half hour and we'll be at the hills.'

'You're right.'

Seaton rode off and gave instructions to the eight men on their side of the wagons and riders. He hoped that the others, who were half a mile away, would catch the idea when he began the attack. He rode back to Archie and Cutler and said, 'We're going to block their way to the track into the hills. Think you can get those beasts of yours to canter a little?'

'We'll have to see.'

It had dawned on Juarez some time earlier that this was no longer a question of whether they were able to turn a profit on the girls, but rather if he and the others would still be alive when the sun rose. That being so, it made no sense at all to hang on to the wagons, which made rapid manoeuvres difficult and swift progress impossible. As Seaton was preparing to block the way into the hills, Juarez was riding up to the men in the wagons. He said, 'It's every man for himself. Forget the cargo; we're saving our skins. How quickly can you men cut the traces and tack up your mounts?'

The reply was to the effect that, given the circumstances, this could be accomplished with great speed.

It was, of course, impossible to cut the traces of the wagons and saddle up the horses without bringing everything to a complete halt. Those in the wagons were profoundly uneasy about this procedure, tormented by the idea that as they were fooling around trying to tack up four horses in the dark, their comrades would ride off and desert them. Under other conditions, this fear might have been a realistic one; none of the comancheros had very finely developed senses of loyalty, compassion, generosity and altruism. Had they been well endowed with such qualities, they would most likely not have taken up as slavers in the first place. In the present instance, though, it was in everybody's interest to stick together rather than separate into two groups. There was more safety in numbers.

'Well,' said Archie to the young man at his side, 'I should say that the knife is about to meet the bone.' The vigilantes had drawn themselves into a long straggling line. As Seaton had hoped, those far away had caught his plan at once and executed a pincer movement, helping to block the way forward for the comancheros. The only way that those men were going to reach the hills now was by fighting their way through a picket line of extremely tough and experienced men.

Seaton's intention was simple and deadly. He had his men dismount and cock their pieces. There were now better than a dozen men with rifles aimed, steady and sure, at the riders who would force their way past them. It would be a massacre if the comancheros carried on down their present path. When riders with pistols face men on the ground with rifles, the outcome is unlikely to favour the men on horseback. However, those riders were desperate now and knew that if they threw down their guns at this point, they would be hanged out of hand. Faced with the Hobson's choice of death by powder and lead or at the end of a rope, they chose to go down fighting. Fifteen riders, firing their pistols wildly as they came on, rode down at a canter on the line of vigilantes.

It was sheer slaughter. Anybody who has ever tried

to fire a forty-five revolver with one hand, while controlling a speeding horse with the other, will know that any sort of accurate marksmanship is quite impossible. Seaton and his vigilance men picked off the riders one by one, calmly taking aim and knocking them down as methodically as though they had been clay pipes in a shooting gallery at the county fair.

The smoke generated from the shooting billowed out and after a short time, obscured the two parties from each other's view. By this time, though, twelve of the comancheros had been shot down, so it did not really signify. Juarez, although having taken his part in the charge, had another purpose entirely and did not propose to cast away his life needlessly in an act of vainglory. By good fortune rather than anything else, he was not killed in the murderous fire being directed at him and his men by the vigilantes. Once the smoke was thick enough, he peeled off to the right and urged his horse on into a gallop. Fifteen riders were never going to be able to gain the relative security of the hills, but one might.

It has to be said that Juarez's motive in abandoning the others and riding hell for leather for the hills were not altogether selfish. He surely wished to save his skin, but the injury which had befallen his sister's only son was much on his mind. The thought of leaving the boy alone in hostile territory, in charge of a lot of young white girls was not a pleasant one. Why, the vigilantes would string him up on the spot should they come across him! It was therefore partly for altruistic reasons that Juarez swerved off and began galloping away from danger.

In all the noise and confusion of battle, what with the crash of gunfire, sound of hoofs, neighing of terrified horses, clouds of smoke and all the members of the posse peering into the gloom to mark a possible target, it was possible that Juarez might just have escaped unnoticed. He so very nearly succeeded and if it were not for the fact that Brent Cutler did not have a rifle, then he probably would have done so. As it was, while those around him were blasting away and even Archie was firing his pistol at the oncoming horsemen, Cutler happened to turn to his left at just the right time to catch a glimpse of a lone rider, plunging through the darkness and likely to be lost from sight given another moment. The others were fully engaged with the task in hand and it would have been absurd to tug at somebody's sleeve and ask what he should do for the best. The long, sleepless night had given everything a dream-like air and so, without anybody taking the least notice, Cutler walked over to where the horses were and mounted up. Then he set off at a canter after the rider he had spotted.

All through their ride that night, Mark Seaton had been brooding about the hanging of Brent Cutler's father. He recalled it vividly and knew that even at the time, he had been uneasy about the business. In retrospect, it had been mighty slick, the way those

bonds had supposedly been found on the man's property. Now, this same man's son had been despatched
to displace Seaton with a sheriff. Well, he had to allow
that there was a measure of poetic justice there and no
mistake! He liked the look of the young man and felt
guilty and ashamed to think of the madness which had
seized him and impelled him to an act of what would
have been tantamount to murder.

Seaton saw, from the corner of his eye, the Cutler
boy skipping over to the horses and mounting up.
Then he caught sight of a fleeting shadow, just on the
edge of his vision, and knew that the boy was chasing
after one of those scoundrels who was about to escape.
Making an exasperated clucking sound, Seaton too
went over to the horses. He couldn't let this green
young lawyer go up alone against one of this band of
cut-throats! So it was that while the others were con-
centrating on finishing off the last of the men who had
mounted their doomed charge, three men rode off,
one after the other, towards the hills.

The end of the mad adventure came with shocking
abruptness. Juarez was tantalizingly close to the track
into the hills, when his mount put a foot in a prairie
dog's hole and he went sailing over her head. His
reactions were not impaired by this sudden accident,
because even as he was rolling on the ground, he was
drawing his pistol and taking aim at the two riders who
were now bearing down. He had to decide in a fraction
of a second at which of the two he would fire first. By

blind chance, he chose Seaton, whose own gun was already in his hand. It was a lucky shot for Juarez, but quite the reverse for the leader of the vigilance men, for the ball took him through the chest and as his horse reared in fright at the sound of the shot so close at hand, Seaton slipped backwards from the saddle, landing heavily.

Cutler was so nervous that he was barely able to pull his piece and draw down on the man now lying in front of him. When he had done so, though, and before the echo of Juarez's shot had died away, he emptied the gun at the comanchero, loosing off all five chambers in quick succession. It only needs one bullet to kill a man and luckily, two of Cutler's wild shots struck home; one in the man's shoulder and the other straight into an eye. Although he was unused to such things, it looked to the young lawyer as though the man on the ground was dead. He got down from the saddle and went over to where Mark Seaton lay.

Kneeling down, Cutler said, 'Is there anything I can do for you, sir?'

Seaton coughed and a trickle of blood, black in the pale moonlight, trickled down his chin. He said painfully, 'You can give me your forgiveness, son. For everything.'

'Lord, that's nothing, Mr Seaton. I'm thinking that you didn't know that my father was a lawman. From what I hear, he was set up.'

'It's too late for to do anything, but I'm sorry. Sorry

that I took against you as well. Reach inside my jacket here. There's your papers.'

Reluctantly, Cutler did as the other had told him and found his letters of introduction and other documents. Clearly, Mark Seaton had not wished to run the risk of anybody else catching sight of them. To his horror, Cutler saw that the papers were besmeared with blood.

The effort of talking was proving costly to the wounded man, because he was panting now and his face was haggard and drawn with pain. Cutler said, 'Don't tire yourself. Can I make you more comfortable?'

'You're a true Christian, son. More so than me, maybe. I hope you do well in life.'

Although his experience of battlefields and injuries was not extensive, Brent Cutler could tell by the quantity of blood which was escaping from the injured man's mouth, that he was gravely, perhaps even mortally, wounded. Seaton's eyes were closed now and his breathing was less stertorous. Then, he suddenly came to again and stared searchingly into Cutler's face. He whispered, 'I've wronged you. You and yours. Sorry.' Then, as Brent Cutler watched, the man took one last convulsive gulp of air and exhaled slowly and fully. He did not draw breath again.

Although he had seen his own father die, being so close to a man as he expired seemed somehow more dreadful and to his surprise and chagrin, Cutler found that tears were running down his cheeks. Why he should feel so strongly at the death of the man who had been instrumental in lynching his father was, to Brent Cutler, something of a mystery.

CHAPTER 11

The aftermath of any event that involves the death of many men is apt to be a melancholy business. There were eighteen corpses to be dealt with after what became known in later years as, 'The Battle of the High Peaks'. It was the bloodiest incident to take place in that region since the end of the war, although fortunately it did not delay the admission of the territory to statehood six months later.

Apart from Mark Seaton, one other member of the posse had been killed by a stray bullet. With all the lead flying about that night, it was hardly a surprise that at least one ball had found its lodging place in the breast of one of the vigilantes. Jack Carlton was disposed to assume command of the outfit now that Seaton had breathed his last. Carlton was feeling pretty braced with the outcome of the night's events. From all that he was able to apprehend, every one of the comancheros was dead, which meant that nobody would be likely to identify him as having had dealings with them at any stage. This was a great relief. Almost as good was the fact that Seaton now lay dead. Not only would he not have to cosy up to that pious son of a bitch, but Carlton guessed that as the dead man's confidant and friend, he might be in with a chance of stepping into his shoes as head of the safety committee.

As everything was being sorted out, dawn was breaking above the mountains. Archie, who most of those present appeared to know and trust, said, 'I mind we ought to go up and look over the camp of those scallawags. Make sure there's none of 'em still around.'

'A fine idea, Mr Carmichael ...' began Jack Carlton, in a bright and cheerful voice.

Archie looked at him coldly and said, 'Don't bother talkin' to me like I'm soft in the head, son. You needn't think on steppin' into no dead man's shoes, neither.'

Some of those present observed that Carlton blushed like a schoolgirl at this and drew their own conclusions. The old man's scheme was sensible and so they all mounted up and set off up the track. Jack Carlton had a face like thunder, wondering where that old goat got off, speaking to him so.

They stumbled across a pitiful sight when once they reached the hollow where the comancheros had been based. Eleven cold, frightened and bedraggled girls, some of them no more than mere children, had spent the whole night in the open, exposed to the pouring rain. All were shivering and some were weeping with terror. They had heard the shooting and did not know what to expect when this hard-looking bunch of men rode up.

The men of the posse looked down at the piteous spectacle and their hearts were consumed with burning rage at the sort of men who could treat help-less young women so. All of them had children of their own; some had daughters of about the same age as these girls. A number dismounted and went over to reassure them that they were now safe and that no harm would befall them. If the vigilance men had up to this point any qualms or misgivings about the mas-sacre in which they had lately taken part, it wanted only the sight of those helpless children to dispel any such emotions.

They moved gently among the girls, taking their own coats off and draping them around the shoulders of those who were in greater need of them than their owners. It was while engaged in this activity, that they stumbled, quite literally, across the youngster who had earlier been injured by the mine which Archie and Cutler had sprung. He was huddled on the muddy ground, in a fever, trembling violently as though he had the ague.

When it became known that one of the bandits who had reduced the young girls to their pitiful state was still breathing, there were murmurs of anger and one or two men looked round to see if there might perhaps be a tree conveniently near at hand. Even in his distressed condition, and with only one eye to guide him, Juarez's nephew was not about to die without a fight. He caught sight of Jack Carlton and pointed a quivering finger at him, crying, 'Ask your fine friend about this. Who brought us our food? Who supplies powder and guns to such as us?'

Despite his horror at discovering that one of those who had seen him come to the camp was still living, Carlton carried things off well enough. He said contemptuously, 'You little snake, you won't save your neck by telling a heap of foolish lies. You'll answer for this! Slaving, indeed. I never heard the like and so close to our own town as well. I tell you, boy, it's all up with you now.'

A few of the men stirred uneasily and one or two looked sideways at Carlton in a curious fashion. There had on occasion been speculation about his not infrequent trips out into the wild with wagons laden with the Lord knew what. Perhaps sensing this, Carlton said, 'I say we deal with this rogue, here and now. What say we hang him as soon as we find a tree?'

'There'll be no hanging of anybody today.' Carlton looked round in astonishment to see who had spoken in such a calm and authoritative manner and found himself facing a young man of perhaps twenty or twenty-five years of age.

'Who the Deuce are you,' asked Carlton, 'to be laying down the law round here?'

'I am the law,' said Brent Cutler quietly.

Unobtrusively, Archie Carmichael moved to the side of his young friend and laid his hand on the hilts of his pistol. He said, 'I'd strongly recommend as you all hear what this fellow has to say.'

'Who the devil are you?' asked Jack Carlton in an ugly voice, staring at Cutler. 'I don't mind that I even know your face. You ain't from hereabouts, I'll be bound.'

'I'm from the District Attorney's office in Pharaoh. My name's Brent Cutler. I've come to help your town make arrangements for proper law. There'll be no more lynchings here.'

Carlton had one last card to lay down. He said, 'You're the rascal who killed Ezra Stannard. We were warned about you. Truth is, some of us were looking to take care of you lately. What have you to say to that?'

Without speaking, Cutler removed from inside his jacket the letters of authority given to him by his office in Pharaoh. He said, 'You're all welcome to examine these at your leisure when we get back to Greenhaven. Meantime, those poor girls look like they need warmth and food rather than us standing here disputing.'

There was something so calm and assured about the young man's manner, that none of those present really doubted that he was who and what he said he was. Some had met him in the bar of the *Lucky Man* not twelve hours since and knew that he had been vouched for by Archie. But as he had said, the first and most urgent priority was to get the poor girls to shelter before they caught their death of cold.

At first, there was some doubt about the neatest and most humane means of transporting the frightened youngsters to town. Then somebody recollected the two wagons and four riders rode off to see if something might be effected in that direction. It proved possible to jury-rig harnesses to the wagons by lashing together the cut traces and supplementing them with pieces of their own tack. Somehow or other the matter was achieved and the girls led down from the hills to where the two wagons were waiting for them. At Cutler's insistence, the wounded boy was also allowed to travel in this way.

Their leader was dead and the Greenhaven safety committee was rudderless and adrift. There was now grave suspicion attached to Jack Carlton and, catching the general mood, he voluntarily withdrew himself to his store and hoped that things would die down. It was certain that there was no appetite to see him appointed to lead the vigilantes. Besides which, everybody felt instinctively that the day of the vigilance men had come to a natural end. Mark Seaton had held the group together by the force of his personality and without him, the remaining men were found to be biddable and not in the least degree averse to seeing a sheriff take over the job of maintaining order in their town. It would perhaps mean taxes of more than the current dollar a month, but that might be a small price to pay for not having to turn out at all hours to tackle crime or disorder.

There was one final point which inclined the men of the town towards accepting tamely the imposition of a regular sheriff. Not all of them were as hot for the Lord as Seaton had been and nor were many of them total abstainers. It might be pleasant to have a bar open past ten at night or even, shocking as the thought had once been, to be able to sup ale on the Sabbath.

Archie Carmichael stayed on in town for a few days to lend his own authority to the enterprise. He was not an educated man, but he surely had a fund of common sense. A few former members of the safety committee also offered their services in organizing the first election ever held in Greenhaven for a municipal post. The man who was voted in was a steady individual who folk reckoned would be up to the job.

It was three weeks before Brent Cutler felt able to leave Greenhaven. He was growing increasingly worried about the horse which he had hired for just seven days in Fort James, wondering if there would be a warrant out for him for rustling by now. But he could not in all conscience have left the town any earlier; not until all the loose ends had been tied up. Letters had been despatched to the families of the girls they had rescued; the bodies of the fallen needed to be collected and there were various other trifling details, which Cutler felt duty-bound to perform. He was keenly aware that he himself had been the catalyst for most of the strange events which had occurred in and around Greenhaven. One minor detail he undertook personally was to turn loose the boy who had lost his eye. Cutler gave him ten dollars and wished him Godspeed. It would have sat ill with him to see such a young fellow dealt with harshly.

On the day before he left the town to head back to Fort James and then pick up the railroad train to Pharaoh, Cutler took a turn round the place to bid one or two people farewell. He called first at the general store, where Jack Carlton was now spending every hour that God sent. He knew fine well that he had had a narrow escape and that any more of his mysterious trips out to the High Peaks would be most unwise. This meant that he was now wholly reliant for his income upon the store and this meant harder work. He no longer had the prestige of being a leading light of the safety committee either. When he saw Cutler entering the store he favoured him with a malevolent glare.

'I just dropped by to let you know that I'm leaving town tomorrow, Mr Carlton,' Cutler told him.

'What's that to me?'

'Only this: you've been lucky. Let's hope that you continue so.' Without waiting for any reply, Cutler turned on his heel and left.

Archie had already gone back to his peculiar cave home and Cutler wished that he might see the old fellow one last time. Howsoever, duty called and he really had to be getting back to the county seat. He had to pay well over the odds for the unauthorized use of the horse for the extra couple of weeks when he finally returned to Fort James.

It was not until he was safely settled on the train to Pharaoh that Cutler really had time to sort out and order all his thoughts and impressions over the last three weeks. His father had been fully exonerated, at least to his own satisfaction. His mother and sisters would be glad to know that, at any rate. His feelings about Mark Seaton were complex and hard to understand. It was fairly certain that Seaton had believed his father to be guilty and that others had fabricated the evidence which led to his lynching. By the time he'd left Greenhaven, Cutler had picked up enough scraps of information to discover that Seaton had also been planning to see him lynched as well. Despite this, he could not find it in his heart to bear a grudge against the dead man. Seaton had lived an upright life, according to his own lights, and had probably done more good than ill.

To his surprise and pleasure, the very same conductor was on the train as on the journey down to Fort James. The old man recognized Cutler and said, 'Well, and how did you find it in Greenhaven? You enjoy yourself?'

'I don't know that I'd say exactly that I enjoyed myself, no,' said Cutler, 'but it was certainly a lively and interesting time.'

'Lively?' exclaimed the conductor, 'lordy, the place

must have changed somewhat since last I was there!'

'I think that the changes are going to continue,' said Cutler. 'Leastways, I'm hopeful that that'll be the case.'